MR

By

Angelia
Vernon
Menchan

Be Blessed Angelia Vernon Menchan

1

MAMM PRODUCTIONS

www.angeliavmenchan.com
http://acvermen.blogspot.com
http://mammproductions.blogspot.com

Cover Design by Maurice K. Menchan

ISBN: 0-9787835-9-X

This book is dedicated in it's entirety to the women I love most...my mama Ora Lee Vernon RIP and my granddaughter Amira Jameela Menchan...

"Cinnamon what are you going to do about Brown?" Cinnamon stared out at the lake surrounding her home. Malcolm Black, her best friend since high school and former lover stood several yards behind her, asking a question she wasn't prepared to answer. She and William Brown had been married over thirty years and as with most marriages there had been ups and downs. Brown had been involved in a series of affairs, Cinnamon and Black had been embroiled in a love affair a couple of years ago. However, for the past eighteen months, she and Brown had focused on being faithful. Brown had fallen off the wagon. She had promised him almost two years ago that if he compromised their marriage again she would divorce him. She had also promised Malcolm she would become his wife if that ever occurred. He had been living a celibate lifestyle waiting for her.

Turning to him, she looked into his handsome, dark chocolate-face. It saddened him to see the pain on her beautiful, toffee-colored face. He loved her more than anything in the world and he wanted her for his own. He'd warned Brown, his friend, on more than one occasion.

"What would you have me do Malcolm? I told him to leave our home and he has. Now I need some time to pray and ask God to guide me on this."

"I understand, but, Cinnamon, you know how I feel about you and I want to marry you, make you my wife…"

"Malcolm, I know and when I marry again, you know it will be you. But right now my life is chaotic. My husband, the father of my children, has decided to have another affair. The husband of the woman decided I needed to know, he also decided to try and blackmail me, once he heard about my books, so what I pray is you're patient with me."

"Are you considering staying with him, again?" She could hear the pain in his voice.

"No, I'm not, but I need to plan what I'm going to do. I've been married almost thirty-two years. I need to find a way to tell my kids. Aura probably already knows. As the premier attorney in Center City, she might. Muhammad is planning to get married in two months and though Amy is only two years old, she loves her Papoo. I love you Malcolm and a part of me wishes I had been a better woman two years ago."

"Better how?"

"I wish that instead of having an affair with you, I had left Brown at that time, allowing him to carry on with Khadijah, but I thought I knew best. As stupid as it may sound, I really thought that when he gave up traveling he would be faithful. But, why would he? He has a wife who has looked the other way for decades, taking him back and forgiving him over and over, so now, I finally have what I deserve. Not only that but I openly ran around with you and we're still close. My guess is that Brown probably doesn't believe we aren't still sexual."

Walking over, he pulled the woman he had loved for almost forty years into his arms. Immediately she started crying. His heart broke, because it took a lot to bring her to tears.

"It would be nice if you waited until the ink was dry on the decree before you moved into my house." Cinnamon and Malcolm pulled apart at the sound of William Brown's voice. Malcolm stared at his friend, choosing to say nothing. Cinnamon walked over to her husband, getting close to his face.

"William Brown, this is my home, it was bought with Dubois money. Please give me my key and leave!" He flinched at her words, she had never mentioned the fact that the home they lived in had been hers when they married, that and acres of land.

"Cinnamon, Brown, I'm going to leave now. Cinnamon if you need me, call." Malcolm prepared to depart.

"That won't be necessary Malcolm, William is leaving." Looking from his wife to his friend, William Brown stood his ground. Malcolm nodded to him, placing a kiss on the side of Cinnamon's mouth, before walking out.

Chapter Two

"So what are you planning to do Cinnamon, move him in my house?" Brown sat down, staring up at his wife. It was hard to look at all the pain in her eyes, pain he had caused.

"William, why are you here?"

"You're my wife, this is my home."

"I have asked you to leave."

"For how long?"

"Forever..." Pain and fear raced in his heart.

"How's that possible? We have been through so much together. I made another mistake..."

"No William, you made a decision. I told you when you decided to give up the Atlanta office that I wouldn't go through this again. I meant that. I just have to figure out a way to tell the children. I can't do this any more."

"Is it because you have a backup plan? Your Black Knight is waiting in the wings. So are the two of you going to marry downtown in the square and make a fool of me?" Startled laughter flew from Cinnamon's throat.

"Is that what this is about, your pride? Is that why we're still married, to keep me from marrying Malcolm?"

"I love you, I've always loved you, but you've always been a lot of work. I allowed you your little indiscretion. You made love to him right up under my nose and I looked the other way. I didn't want to lose you, but I won't allow you to leave me and make a fool of me and all we have worked to have."

"Negro, you don't have a choice. I don't think you know who you're dealing with. And for the record Malcolm and I didn't have an indiscretion. We had a love affair, he loves me and I love him!" White hot pain ran through Brown at Cinnamon's words. He was shocked.

"So how do you expect me to only be with you, when you're with him?"

"William, you were sleeping all over for almost thirty years before Malcolm ever touched me. And in almost two years, Malcolm and I haven't shared so much as a kiss. He hasn't had his hands on me or any other woman. He loves ME that much! Your idea of love seems to be ownership of me, while screwing someone else. How do you think I felt when that man showed up at my door with pictures of you butt naked *inside* his wife?" He cringed at her words.

"I'm sure if I had wanted to, I would have been able to have photos of you with Malcolm Black!"

"As usual you're avoiding the real issue! I wish you had, then we could have resolved this mess years ago."

"What mess is that, is that what you consider our marriage, a mess?"

"B, it is a mess..." His heart surged at her calling him 'B,' that was an affectionate name she had called him since they were children. "William, we have created a mess. For over two decades we traveled the world, in every port you had your little, 'things,' as a woman, a wife and the mother of your children, I chose to look the other way. What we had seemed to transcend that. However, once we moved back to Florida, I truly thought that was all over. I was so busy getting Muhammad through school, taking care of my dying mother and working, I couldn't see what was going on. And Malcolm was there for me at every juncture. I didn't know his feelings for me or acknowledge mine for him; but he took care of me when no one else did. I remember all those lonely nights I sat with mama and you were God knows where, doing the devil knows what. He came by with food, books and conversation. I never meant to love him, but it seemed to become inevitable. After he confessed his feelings to me, you practically forced us together, inviting him into our lives, our home. B, he told you how he felt and he also told you he would never go away, not once you invited him in. Now, I understand, you were having an affair with Khadijah and my being with Malcolm just evened the playing field in your mind. What you didn't count on was how much he loved me! You are unable to understand that. For almost two years he and I have been running the Learning Center, we have been friends... that's it, just friends. However, your latest little indiscretion changes everything. William, I want to be loved, cared for and honored

10

by a man who places me first after God. William Brown, it seems you aren't that man." Swallowing down a lump, Brown stared at his wife. He didn't know what to say. There was nothing he could say.

"William, please leave, I need some peace. I need you to come by tomorrow so we can talk to Aura."

"What are you planning to tell her?"

"The truth… that her mom and dad are separating after over three decades of marriage and that while we love her and each other, it isn't enough to sustain us any longer. She's almost thirty years old, she'll be fine."

"What will we tell our families?"

"I only have Aunt Gladys to tell. You can tell your family whatever you want to, I don't care."

Not knowing what else to say he reluctantly walked from his home. His heart felt as though it were going to fly from his chest. He never thought Cinnamon would make the decision to divorce him. They had been through so much.

God, please give me the strength to deal with all of this. I know you frown on divorce, but God I can't go on like this. I have stayed faithful and true to that man to the best of my abilities. I know I stepped out of your will, when I was sexually involved with Malcolm but God I also know I have asked for and received forgiveness from you. I'm going to need you ever so desperately to get me through this. I love William, but I'm too tired to go through this again. Amen.

What in the world am I going to do? I don't know what I was thinking getting involved with that woman. For the past year, our lives have been almost platinum. I know Cinnamon has been true to me even though she was still close to Malcolm Black. We enjoyed helping raise our granddaughter and it's been so awesome. God, why in the world did I allow myself to fall once again into the trap of my own lusts? I can't imagine getting up everyday without Cinnamon in my life. I love and need her and God, though I'm ashamed to admit it, I can't live in this town and watch the two of them. It would kill me.

Chapter Three

Aura Brown wondered who in the world could be knocking on her door at ten p.m. on a Friday night. She had gotten her daughter, Amy, in bed about ten and she was exhausted. After working a twelve hour day at her law firm and taking care of a cranky baby she simply wanted to have a glass or two of wine and sleep in tomorrow morning until Amy woke her. Now that her firm was successful, she could finally afford to not work on Saturdays. Peeking through the keyhole she could see her dad standing in her doorway. Her heart raced, wondering if something had happened to her mom or her brother. Snatching the door open she was startled to smell liquor on her dad's breath. She was even more surprised to see his shirt wrinkled and his tie askew.

"What's wrong dad, is mom okay? Has Muhammad called?" Walking in around her and plopping down on her grey leather couch, he mumbled, "She put me out..."

"What?" Before he could answer she walked into the kitchen to start a pot of coffee. When she walked back into the room she could see tears flowing freely from his eyes. She sat down next to him, handing him a cup of strong, espresso laced coffee.

"Dad what's wrong?"

"Your mama put me out, she has finally left me." Aura wasn't at all startled, she knew of her father's history.

13

"What happened, this time, dad?" Shame appeared in his heart at her words.

"I don't even know how to tell you. But, I'm afraid this is it. I've never seen her like that. She told me a couple of years ago that she would leave me. I just didn't think she ever would. Now that she has someone..."

"Dad, I don't know what to tell you other than to pray. God ultimately decides what will happen. But I'm going to say this, mama has been a better woman than me, I'd have left you years ago." Pain rushed through him at his daughter's words, pain and shame.

"I know. I just don't know what I'm going to do. I guess you aren't willing to talk to your mom on my behalf."

"Daddy, I'm not getting involved like that. I love you and mama and I'll support whatever you decide. I sure don't want the two of you to get divorced, but I won't take sides. Mama called today to tell me she wanted the three of us to meet tomorrow night for dinner. I guess she's planning to say something then."

"She didn't say anything about all of this?

"Not a word, but that's how mama is. Look dad, you need to go and sleep in the spare bedroom, you're in no shape to drive and maybe this will all look better in the morning." Aura feelings went from tired to exhausted.

"Thank you, I have another question. How would you feel if your mama married Malcolm Black?" Aura's face flushed at her dad's words. She didn't know how to answer him without hurting his feelings.

"Dad, I think you're jumping the gun. Right now mama is still married to you. Now get some sleep and we'll talk about it in the morning.

*****

The next morning after her ten mile run, Aura returned to find her dad sitting at her kitchen table with Amy on his lap. He looked as though he hadn't had a bit of sleep. He'd made coffee and was feeding Amy applesauce.

"Papoo got sad face, mommy…" Amy used her little hand trying to brush away the sadness. Aura's heart crumbled at the sight of her over two hundred pound dad sucking back sobs. Taking Amy from his lap, she sat her down on the floor. Walking to her dad she sat down close to him.

"Why, daddy..? I know I asked you a couple of years ago. But if you love mama as you say why go there again, especially now?"

"I wish I knew baby, I do love your mama, but I never felt like I measured up. When we got married I felt like the pauper marrying the princess. She tried so hard with me, but every time I felt that way, it was like if I didn't do something I would jump out of my skin. My something turned out to be other women. For the past year it has been so good

15

between us, especially with the baby at the house. But it seems that when she told me she was going to start her own tutoring center, all of the old insecurities crept back in and there I was again."

"Dad, are you competing with mama?"

"I guess you could call it that. She's so damn powerful, everything she touches turns to gold. For years she acted like she didn't even want a career. Then she became an award winning teacher. Then after she retired from teaching she started with that magazine. Everywhere I went I had to hear about her articles, *'Cinnamon Speaks.'* Then when she wrote those books, she was a celebrity and I felt like I was in the background. Of course she helped Malcolm turn the Learning Center into a success, now she wants to branch off and start the 'Empowerment Place.' I don't know…" He knew how petty he sounded.

"Well, dad, all I know is, mama took care of you, us, grandma, the aunts and everyone else who ever needed her. She even takes care of Amy most days. It just seems right that she should be allowed to do this. Daddy, this isn't about you."

"I know. Look, I'm going into my office today. I'll see you at five at the house. Thanks for last night." Aura leaned over kissing her dad on his face. She wanted to call her mom, but she knew Cinnamon would tell her when she was ready.

Chapter Four

"Hello." Cinnamon's tired voice sounded on the phone.

"Hey Lady, are you okay this morning. I wanted to call you last night but I know you and Brown needed to talk." Malcolm's concern was clear in his voice.

Cinnamon walked around her garden, absentmindedly watering. It seemed that since she had spoken to Roger Lee she'd been in a fog.

"I'm okay. Brown wasn't here too long after you left. I'm taking care of the garden. I'm meeting with Aura and Brown tonight. What are you doing today?"

"I don't have any plans. Jock is with his father this weekend. Can I see you tonight?"

"I would like that. Maybe I can meet you at our cabin at nine o'clock. Is that okay?"

"I would love that. Cinnamon, I love you."

"I know." She gently placed the phone in the cradle.

****

Black wasn't surprised to see Brown walk around to the back of his home. In fact he had been expecting him. After speaking to Cinnamon he had done work around his home. For the past half hour

17

he had simply been sitting, waiting. He watched his best friend and husband of the woman he loved walk towards him. He felt a mix of emotions, sadness at his friend's pain, sorrow that he had somehow contributed to it but mostly he was glad that what had occurred hadn't been instigated by him. It had been very difficult for people to understand how the two men had remained so close, particularly during the time when Black and Cinnamon had been so intimate. Arriving at the patio Brown sat down after retrieving a bottle of beer from the mini refrigerator. For several minutes the two men were quiet. Brown was first to break the silence.

"So are you planning a celebration party?" Black could hear the pain in his friend's voice.

"Man, it isn't even like that. I have stayed in my corner for almost two years. I did everything I could to stay out of your marriage. But I told you that if the day came when you messed up again and if Cinnamon chose to leave you, I would be there for her. Man I love you like a brother, but I love her more than I love my own life. What happened?"

"Man, I don't even know how it all happened. A few months ago when Cinnamon told me about her new venture, it made me mad. It seemed like she was always doing something. About the same time Jennifer Lee came to work in my office. One thing led to another."

"Man, don't tell me you fell for the Lee's bag of tricks?"

"What does that mean?"

"Man, they have blackmailed so many people. Roger is as old as me and that girl is not even thirty, for the past ten years they have been setting her up with men with money, taking photos and moving on. Is that what happened?" Brown swallowed down rage, realizing he had been set up.

"Yes, but they didn't come to me. He took the photos to Cinnamon, asking her for fifty grand for the originals. When I got home she threw them in my face, telling me to leave."

"Please tell me there weren't actual photos of…"

The look on Brown's face confirmed it. Black shuddered at the pain that must have caused Cinnamon.

"So, do you plan to marry my wife?" Black's stare met Brown's head on.

"I absolutely do. Man, I love you as much as I love my flesh and blood, but if I get the opportunity to make her Mrs. Black I will. Nothing changes that." For several minutes the two men sat in silence.

"I thought you didn't want to tarnish her image."

"Marrying me won't tarnish her image. Man you messed up after she told you what would happen. I also told you I knew you would mess up again. Your dalliances have been your power for years. It seems, my brother, you have rendered yourself powerless."

"I don't plan to go away quietly."

"I didn't expect you to. But heed my words, neither me, those kids of yours or anyone else who loves that woman will allow you to hurt her. Brown, don't make this, you or her thing, because you stand to lose. The only people in Center City who will support you will be your family, and I suspect they'll think you're a fool." Draining the last dregs of beer from his bottle, Brown stood, nodding at his friend and nemesis before walking to his truck. Black silently prayed they all survived what was ahead. One thing he knew for sure is that he was going to fight for Cinnamon this time. She would become Mrs. Black.

Chapter Five

Brown drove around aimlessly for several hours. Shock and pain permeated his pores. Last night when he had looked at the photos Cinnamon had thrown in his face he was ashamed. He had been with the woman one time and this had occurred. He wondered why they hadn't approached him. He would have given them the fifty grand, gladly, to get them away. But they had chosen Cinnamon. He knew it was time to pay the piper. Looking at his watch he saw he had a few hours before his meeting with Cinnamon and Aura, he decided to go talk to his parents.

****

Sitting across from his aging parents he was hurt to see the shame on his father's face. His mother wasn't a big fan of Cinnamon, and thought her kids could do no wrong, but his dad looked genuinely distressed at what he had shared with them.

"Son, how could you allow this to happen? You have a beautiful wife and a great life, how could you? I thought everything was wonderful." Unable to meet his dad's eyes he turned to his mother. She smiled, grabbing his hands.

"Well son, it lasted way longer than I ever thought. Cinnamon has always thought too highly of herself. What is she going to do now, marry that millionaire?"

"Jackie, now don't go starting mess. This boy just told you his wife is going to leave him and you already throwing stones." Jefferson Brown wasn't surprised at his wife's words, she had been complaining to him about Cinnamon since their son married her. "Cinnamon is a good woman and mother, William should be happy to have her. And that girl ain't got to marry no millionaire... she's probably worth millions herself. Her mama and all those aunts of hers have been leaving her land and money for years."

"All I know is I have seen her running all over town with that Malcolm Black and I know they're more than friends. She's been playing around with him out in the open. And mark my words just as sure as sugar is sweet she'll marry him." Jackie Brown stood, walking over to the sink. Brown and his dad walked out to the garage.

"Son, don't listen to your mama. Cinnamon is a good woman. She's as pretty as she can be and she has worked hard to give you nice kids and a beautiful home. Don't let her go."

"Dad, I don't want to, but I've messed up big this time. She told me she would leave me if I messed up again and now I have. Mama's right. Cinnamon will marry Black if we get divorced. He's been waiting in the wings for years."

"Son, I suspect you're right, that's why you shouldn't have given her or him a reason. Do the kids know?"

"I told Aura last night. We're all supposed to go to California in a couple of months for

Muhammad's wedding. I suspect his mama will tell him."

"No, you need to tell that boy. I suspect you told Aura."

"I did, she's usually more tolerant of me, Muha loves me but he's protective of his mama."

"Most boys are. Will, I love you, but you should have grown up a long time ago. I knew about some things and I excused them as a man being a man. We've all had our little mistakes. But you're over fifty now." Looking at his father, Brown could only nod.

"Do you think she will really leave me?"

"Son, I don't know, but if she told you she would, I expect she will, she doesn't say anything she doesn't mean. I sure will miss her. She has been an asset to this family." Nodding at his dad, he walked back in to his mom. She stood at the sink washing greens, in her early seventies, she still cooked everyday.

"So mama what do you think I should do." Peering at him over her glasses, she told him, "I told you years ago to keep her away from that Black. I watched him sniffing around her even when her mama was alive. And when you started bringing him in your home, I warned you. But you didn't listen to me. A fool could see how much he wanted her. And I guess she wanted him back."

"Mama, I know you want to blame Cinnamon but I did this. I have been cheating on my wife for years. She stood by me and loved me through it all. Mama I messed up, not her. She could have left me for Malcolm years ago, but she chose me."

"Then I don't know what to tell you Will. All you can do is pray and hope she comes to her senses. I told her years ago that a man will be a man. A woman just has to be patient. Your daddy was the same way. I waited him out, now things couldn't be better. God works in his own time."

Kissing his mother's cheek he knew at least one person was on his side, but it didn't provide much comfort. He wanted his wife on his side.

Chapter Six

Cinnamon spent the morning praying. Her heart ached from the sight of those pictures. She couldn't get the graphic images out of her mind. She knew that if someone had shown her something like that years ago, she would have already left Brown. It was one thing to suspect, something else to know, but there was no comparison to seeing with her own eyes. Looking in the mirror, she could see the sadness in her own eyes. She was a tall toffee colored woman. Her light brown eyes were oval shaped and clear. Many people proclaimed her ten years younger but today she felt every one of her almost fifty three years. She had gotten Ed, her hair stylist, to come by to cut her hair and according to him she looked even younger with her two inch curls. Dressed in a short black, sleeveless dress and black ballerina flats she felt ready for a funeral. Hearing the doorbell chime, she glanced at her watch. It was only four-thirty. Walking over she saw her beautiful daughter standing in the doorway with a cake from Starbucks in her hand.

"Do I get a new key? I tried my key in the lock and it wouldn't budge." Kissing her daughter's face, Cinnamon smiled at the censure in Aura's words.

"Of course, now can I have that cake or do you want to get right to getting in my business?" Placing the cake down on the coffee table, Aura turned to look at her mother. Even though Cinnamon was five feet and ten inches, Aura towered over her by two inches and she was even taller in two inch heels. She thought her mom had never looked lovelier and to the unpracticed eye the pain didn't show.

Cinnamon had been raised to never let them see her sweat.

"Are you okay Cinnamon Bun? You look really pretty in your black dress but I can see your pain."

Swallowing down tears, Cinnamon wanted to bawl in her daughter's arms, but she didn't know how. Other than with her best friend, Alexandra and Malcolm she had been the strength for everyone else. Alexandra was out of the country on business for two weeks.

"Not really baby, I don't want to add to your burden." Sitting down and pulling her mom close to her, Aura rubbed her soft curly hair. The gentle touch caused the tears to flow freely.

"I'm so sorry, but I can't do it any longer, I can't go through this charade, pretending I don't know my husband is a serial philanderer. Aura that man placed photos in my hand."

"Mama, tell me that's not true."

"I wish I could but it is. Actual photos of my husband and his wife, butt naked, sexually graphic pictures. I thought I had felt all the pain I could but I can't explain how I felt. I guess your daddy failed to mention that." *No he was more concerned about you and Mr. Black.*

"No, he didn't mention that at all. I'm so sorry mama, I'll support whatever you decide and as I told daddy I would have left him long ago."

"As you told your dad…"

"Yes, ma'am, he came over last night as drunk as Cooter Brown. He asked if I thought you would leave him."

"Now that's exactly what I meant. William Brown cheats at everything. I asked him, implicitly not to say anything to you or your brother until we could talk to you together. And he gets up and goes to tell you the first chance he gets. I guess he's trying to get you on his side."

"Mama, I'm not on anyone's side. I told daddy I would hate for you to get divorced, but mama I understand. Life is too short for that. Mama all you need to know is I love you and will support you completely, whatever you decide to do. Have you spoken to Pastor Walker?"

"No, I haven't, I really don't want to talk to him. He and your dad golf together and they are friends. I don't know if he can be impartial. No one is better at bringing the word, but I have always felt that Pastor Walker is something of a chauvinist. The way I feel right now, I would run the risk of saying the wrong thing." Before Aura could respond they heard the doorbell ring. Cinnamon closed her eyes, saying a prayer before walking to the door. Brown stood at the door feeling lost because he'd had to ring the doorbell to the house he'd been living in for years. His heart filled with more pain when his wife opened the door. He could see that her usually clear eyes had red lines running through them. He wanted to take her in his arms but her posture told him not to. Walking into the house he could smell home-cooked food. His stomach grumbled, reminding him he had barely eaten in several days. He was startled to see Aura had arrived before him. However, he was pleased when she walked over to kiss his face.

"Where's your car?" he asked his daughter.

"I parked it in the garage." He watched his wife sit down beside his daughter, her eyes fastened on him. He could barely look at her. For several minutes they sat in silence, finally Cinnamon broke the silence.

"Aura, we wanted you to come over today, so we could tell you that we, your dad and I, are officially separating." Tears were clear in her voice. In an odd way that heartened Brown, it indicated separating from him wasn't an easy choice for her. He marveled at how lovely she looked, even with sad, watery eyes, she looked like Aura's older sister, rather than her mother. Even with the abundance of silver that had appeared amongst her jet black curls. It looked as though a quarter of her hair had grayed overnight. "Speaking for myself, I want you to know this has no bearing on you, Muhammad or Amy. It's simply that I'm tired of living the way I have been. I have made many mistakes in my life and my marriage, but I never stopped loving my husband, children or honoring my commitments." Swallowing down a lump, she continued with what had to be the hardest words she had ever uttered as a mother. "Though, I'm sure there are those who would beg to differ, considering I had a love affair with Malcolm Black a couple of years ago. But I know God has already forgiven me

28

for that transgression and that has nothing to do with this. I'm simply tired of living a life of hypocrisy. I stand in front of young women every day telling them how to empower themselves, yet I'm living in an un-empowered state." Looking around the room she saw tears in her daughter's eyes and pouring from the eyes of her husband. "Brown…"

"I have nothing to say. I love your mother and want nothing more than to stay married to her until I die. I've made many mistakes and it seems like I have committed the final one. I want you both to know I'll fight to save my marriage." Aura cleared her throat, knowing this was a good place for her to interject.

"I love both of you. Mama, I respect what you're doing and I understand. Dad, I love and respect you also, but I beg you not to do anything *else* to embarrass mama or this family. If mama decides to do something permanent that's her God given right." Her eyes held fast to her dad's, he wanted to look away but was unable to. He knew his daughter was warning him. "Also, I would like to stay out of this. I'll be there for the two of you. However, I won't choose sides. Most importantly I won't represent either of you." Both parents nodded with love and respect.

"Has anyone spoken to Muha?" Aura had spoken to her brother earlier and he hadn't mentioned anything to her. Cinnamon nodded, no.

"I plan to speak to him, as his father I think it's my responsibility."

29

"Brown, I don't mean any harm, but I want to speak to him with you."

"How will we do that? I was going to call him later. Dad thinks he needs to hear it from me first."

"What are you planning to tell him because you jumped the gun to tell Aura and it seems you left out key components? Brown this has nothing to do with our children other than they deserve to know their parents are no longer living together." Glancing at his daughter, Brown cleared his throat.

"I'm sorry. I needed to talk to someone." Getting to her feet, Aura decided to leave.

"I'm going to fix a couple of plates for me and Amy and I'm going home. Just remember I love you both." Leaning over she grabbed her bag, heading for the kitchen. She planned to prepare the plates and leave from the kitchen through the garage. It was painful to see how hurt her parents were. She also had to admit that if she were going to take sides, it was her mother's. She had never seen her mama look so defeated.

"So are we going to have dinner together?"

"No Brown, however, you are welcome to take the food I prepared. If you want to you can talk to Muha, however, I sent him a ticket to fly down here this weekend. He's coming in on Friday night and flying out on Sunday morning. I simply told him I wanted to see him." Swallowing down a lump he nodded his acceptance.

"That will be fine. If you don't mind, I'm going to fix some food for myself before I leave. Do you need anything?" She nodded no, before walking upstairs. Walking into the kitchen he saw a platter of food sitting on the counter. He knew his daughter had prepared it for him. Looking back into the kitchen where he had enjoyed hundreds of meals and laughter he grabbed his plate walking out.

Cinnamon stood at her bedroom window, looking down at her husband climb into his truck with a plate of food in his hands. Unfiltered, salty tears ran down her cheeks.

Chapter Seven

Black glanced at his watch as he paced around the cabin. It was ten minutes before nine but he was afraid Cinnamon wouldn't show up. They had spent many hours in this cabin, but it had been months since she'd been out here. After vowing to not be sexual with each other, they knew that being alone in an isolated cabin wasn't a good idea. He was very pleased she had suggested it. It indicated she was really going to make a change. A couple of years earlier she had found out about one of Brown's affairs and had opted to stay. Though he hadn't said a word, it had cut him deeply, leaving him feeling like no matter what Brown did, she would stay. Somehow whatever had occurred this time, seemed to be the deal breaker. He had no intentions of pressuring her but he wanted her to keep her word this time. Looking around the cabin, he could see the peach roses she loved and smell the food he had purchased for her. A knock on the door startled him out of his thoughts. Walking to the door he was pleased to see her standing in the door, dressed in black with a startlingly white, silk shawl around her shoulders. Pulling her into the cabin he pulled her into his arms, holding her tightly, she wrapped her arms tightly around him. What neither of them saw was the car pulling unto the deserted property with the lights off.

"Are you okay?" Still holding his love, Black looked at her, delighted that a smile was present in her eyes.

"I am now. It's been a rough patch, but I'm going to get through this." Sniffing the air she could smell garlic, butter and a hint of seafood. Kicking off her shoes, allowing the shawl to slide from her shoulders she walked into the kitchen area. The cabin was a huge open space with all points viewable except the bathroom. Watching her stroll to the kitchen, Black swallowed down the desire that was threatening to overtake him. She peeked into the pots, seeing her favorite soft shell crabs. Turning to Black she saw him peeking out the window.

"Is someone out there?"

"No, I don't think so." He was concerned, because while he didn't see a car or lights his gut instincts told him someone had been out there. Not wanting to scare Cinnamon he kept those thoughts to himself. He walked to the kitchen, where she was ladling food into bowls. Sitting down beside her, they quietly ate while he feasted on her with his eyes. When they were done he walked to the recliner, pulling her into his lap.

"Talk to me…"

"We had dinner with Aura earlier…that went okay. I'm so proud of her, she told us in no uncertain terms that she wasn't taking sides and she wouldn't represent us."

"You should be proud, she's awesome. How's Muhammad taking it?"

"He doesn't know yet. He's coming home on Friday and we plan to tell him then. I'm sure he'll be fine."

"I hope so, those kids love both of you so much and I don't want them to judge you."

"Malcolm, don't worry about that. Aura isn't judging me at all. In fact she told her dad, she would have left him years ago. I also told her tonight in front of Brown that our love affair has nothing to do with this."

"Our love affair, is that what you said?" Turning in his lap as she looked at him, she could feel him becoming aroused.

"That's what it is, isn't it?"

"Umm hmm, Cinnamon you might want to get out of my lap because this is becoming hard for me." His choice of words caused her to laugh without inhibition. It felt good because she hadn't laughed in days.

"Yes it is. That's a good thing, isn't it?" Her voice had become low and throaty.

"I don't know, is it?" Not answering with words she wrapped her lips around his, kissing him fervently. He kissed her back with equal passion. After several minutes he looked at her, his eyes filled with questions. Smiling, she stood up, walking over to the king-sized bed in the middle of the room. He rushed over behind her, urgently undressing her, then undressing himself. Once they were completely undressed he started peppering her with kisses from head to toe....

Waking up Black was startled and pleased to see Cinnamon in his arms. Immediately, their lovemaking started to play in his mind. He hadn't allowed himself to even consider that Cinnamon would allow him to make love to her. He was consumed with joy and pleasure that she had. She looked so beautiful and peaceful, snoring softly. Glancing at the clock he realized it was 2 a.m. He gently shook her.

"Cinnamon…." Sleepily opening her eyes she glanced at him with a smile on her face.

"Huh…"

"It's almost 2 a.m. Don't you need to go home?"

"No, I need to sleep. But if you want me to leave in the wee hours of the morning, I will, otherwise can I go back to sleep. Besides, I am home…" Immediately she was sleeping again. He got up, pulling on his sweatpants. Walking outside he looked around the property, he could see faint tire tracks on the soft dirt. His heart raced in his chest. That confirmed for him that someone had been outside last night. Someone was following Cinnamon.

Four hours later when Cinnamon woke up, she looked around for Malcolm. He was standing at the window looking out.

"What's wrong Black Man?" Turning to her, his heart filled at the sight of her.

"I don't know how to tell you this, but someone followed you here last night. There were fresh tire tracks in the dirt last night that didn't match yours. They appeared to be car tracks. I'm guessing it wasn't Brown, unless he rented a car. The tracks were too small for the tires he has on the Escalade." He waited for worry to mar her face. She simply shrugged her shoulders as she stood up, padding to the bathroom. After she had dressed they sat on the back porch drinking coffee.

"Are you worried at all?"

"Not really, what's the worse that could happen?" In a few hours those words would have deeper meaning.

"I don't know. I just don't feel good about it."

"I feel good." He smiled at her.

"About…"

"About last night, I didn't come over here to mess with your vow of celibacy, but I'm glad I did." Chortling he looked at her.

"Good, I have never felt better in my life. It has been a long time… What's on your agenda today?"

"I'm going to go home, take a shower and go see Aunt Gladys. I need to tell her what's going on before she hears it through the grapevine. Jackie

Brown already knows and she will make it her business to tell my auntie. My mother-in-law isn't my biggest fan.

****

Three hours later, after showering and changing, Cinnamon was on the way downstairs when she heard the doorbell ringing. Walking to answer it, she saw Aura standing with her hand on the buzzer. Her face was all business. Opening the door she walked in thrusting a newspaper in her mom's hands. It was a copy of **'Black News to Use,'** a local tabloid that specialized in sensationalism. Opening it Cinnamon gasped. On the front page was a caption that read, *"Love Nest?"* There was a picture of her standing in the doorway of Black's cabin, her back was to the camera but he was clearly visible. Beneath the caption and pictures were the words: *Who is the lovely, very married, bestselling author visiting the mysterious Black millionaire? Is she doing research for a new book or is this a love den?*

"Oh my God, where in the world did you get this from?" Cinnamon tried to keep the shock out of her voice.

"It's delivered to my office every day. My clients love reading this. Mama is that you? The picture is pretty grainy but that looks like you with Malcolm Black."

Sinking down onto the sofa, Cinnamon nodded her head affirmatively.

"Mama, who do you think did this?" Words failed her. "Do you think dad did this?"

"Baby, I don't know. Maybe, I can't imagine who else would have a motive. However, I can't imagine your dad would want this in the newspapers. I think he would find this embarrassing. I'm so sorry. I had no idea this would show up in the tabloids. They have an ax to grind with me anyway."

"Who does?"

"Gabriel Lemiuex, the owner of this paper. A few years ago when I started to write for *'Black Venue,'* he asked me to write for his paper. I turned him down because I didn't want to write that kind of garbage. They are known for exposing people and tabloid journalism. He called me out, saying I was a traitor, writing for Thane Whitton, who was an outsider. Whoever took this picture, knew where to take it."

"Do you want me to do something?"

"No baby, I don't, it would only add fuel to the fire. I need to go talk to Aunt Gladys. She loves to read trash. She has probably seen me already. Again, I'm sorry."

"Sorry for what mama, for having a love den?" Looking at her daughter she saw Aura's wagging eyebrows and knew she was teasing her. Laughter erupted from both of them. Cinnamon kissed her daughter, telling her to go back to work. Before she could leave the phone rang.

"Hello."

"Did you see that nasty newspaper?"

"Yes, Aura brought it to me. If she hadn't I wouldn't have seen it. How did you see it?"

"When I went to the Center this morning, it was outside with the other newspapers. What do you want me to do?"

"Not a thing. I'm going to talk to my aunt about it. Later on I will be at the Center so we can work on the plans for the 'Empowerment Place'.

"You sound really calm."

"Malcolm, I am calm. I'm sorry it happened. I don't want to embarrass my children or my aunt. I don't even want to embarrass Brown but you know what, it is a love den. I do need a favor though, make sure you install cameras around the property and make sure no one can hook up any cameras inside."

"They're working on the cameras outside and inside now. That place is like Fort Knox, no one can get in there."

"Good, I gotta run, but I'll see you later."

"Cinnamon, I love you."

"I love you…"

Chapter Eight

Cinnamon wasn't surprised to see Aunt Gladys sitting on the screened porch. She knew that not far away was a glass of overly sweet tea, several magazines and newspapers. At eighty-two Aunt Gladys was still a picture of health. She was the only one of the Dubois sisters left, of the original five. Her sister, Sara, had died less than two years earlier. Cinnamon's mother had died almost six years earlier. The others had been dead for years. Hearing the door slam, Gladys looked at her niece in her white sundress and Chanel sunglasses wrapped around her face. With her string-up sandals she looked like a thirty year old. Arriving on the porch, Cinnamon blew bubbles on the side of her aunt's face. That was one of their forms of affection since the days when Cinnamon was a toddler. Like then Gladys pretended to wipe it off, though she loved and treasured it. Plopping down on the swing beside her aunt, Cinnamon picked up the frosty jar of tea sipping from it.

"Girl, put my tea down, you know I don't like people slurping in my stuff." The two women giggled together.

"Auntie Diva, you know you like me drinking behind you. Now go on and fuss at me, so we can get that out the way."

"I'm not going to fuss. I want you to tell me what's going on. Though you as pretty as a picture and giggling, I can tell something is going on."

"How can you tell?"

"Number one, you still got on those movie star glasses, number two it has only been a couple weeks since I saw you and you look like you've lost about ten pounds and number three I know everything." Pulling off her glasses, Cinnamon looked at her aunt.

"I put Brown out of the house."

"What happened?"

"He's not honoring us and I'm tired Auntie." Nodding her head, Gladys picked up her tea, sipping from it. Getting up she walked inside. Placing a slice of lemon pound cake, Cinnamon's favorite, on a saucer, she poured a glass of tea adding lemon to it, the way her niece loved. Walking back outside, she handed the treats to her niece.

"Sweetie, I'm sorry to hear that. I have heard things about him over the years, but I stayed out of it. Someone told me he was fooling around with that African woman but I left ya'll's business alone. Is that it?"

"Yes, auntie, but it isn't her. I have tried really hard to make my marriage work, forever. For the most part it has but I can't put up with the back and forth any more. I was going to leave Brown years ago, but so many things made me stay. My love for him, the kids, the family, so many things, but auntie I'm tired now."

"You are also in love with someone else."

41

"I am auntie. He's so good to me and for me. He loves me like I've never been loved before. But this isn't about him, it's about me and Brown."

"Well, I don't know, seeing as how he's in that newspaper with you, it's about you now." Sighing, Cinnamon turned to look at her aunt.

"Auntie, I'm sorry. Black has had that cottage for years. It is a love den. It's where I meet him, our secret getaway. I hadn't been out there in months, but last night I needed to see him and it seemed like the right place. I had no idea."

"Do you think it was William?"

"At first I did, but after thinking about it, it doesn't make sense. He's usually so private and proud, I can't see him doing it, but I really don't know."

"Does he know?"

"I don't know. Aura brought the paper to me this morning. Malcolm has already seen it. I'm sure he has by now. Auntie I don't really care."

"Good, you shouldn't care. But, I want you to be careful. There are a lot of people in this town who think you have too much and would do anything to cause problems. Just ask God to guide you and stay in prayer. And I'm sorry about you and William. I'm not surprised though. Sara and I used to talk about how much you had endured. The Dubois women aren't known for that kind of loyalty. We would usually pack up and leave a Negro in a minute."

"I know, I guess that also contributed to my staying. Auntie, I was surrounded by strong women, but women who always did it by themselves. And though there was no one I admired more than mama and my aunts there were times when I could see how lonely you all were."

"You were very observant. The Dubois women have always had money and their own stuff, but nothing is like love, nothing in the world. And baby, remember this, you're a good woman, a great mother and you were an awesome wife to William Brown. Do you think you'll marry Malcolm Black?"

"Are you kidding, I sure will, though I would need some recovery time."

"Good, you two sure are suited for each other. So what do the kids think?"

"Aura is fine, Muhammad is coming tomorrow. I don't know how he'll feel, he is such a mama's boy, but he reveres his dad. I'm sure he knows his dad's history and he knows about me and Malcolm. Auntie they're grown and they're going to feel however they're going to feel."

"You're right. So what are you up to these days, other than showing up in newspapers?"

"I'm still working at the Center, but I'm also working on opening the Empowerment Place by the beginning of the year. It's something that mama and I talked about years ago. It's time. I think that's what sent Brown out on his latest venture."

"I don't understand."

"It's pretty simple really. Every time I do something for me, Brown gets weird. I remember when I went back to school both times, he got crazy. He couldn't understand why I needed degrees if he took such good care of me. When I started writing he almost lost his mind, he just couldn't believe it. He just wanted me to take care of him and the kids. Now that I'm getting ready to do something else he started acting up again. Thinking about it he probably was behind those photos. He might think they will stop me from doing the tutoring. Maybe thinking it will tarnish my image. I don't know. Auntie, I got to go, but I'll see you in a couple of days." Kissing her aunt, she strolled down the sidewalk. Gladys Dubois watched her niece, thinking, *He's making a huge mistake, he don't even want to mess with her. He's messing with me when he messes with her and he doesn't want to feel my wrath. I need to talk to Mr. William Brown.*

Chapter Nine

Aura walked into her father's office. Storming past the receptionist, she walked into his office. He was on the phone when she entered. Seeing the look on her face he ended his call. Throwing the newspaper on the desk, she looked at him, he looked at it, then back at his daughter. His face showed nothing, not even surprise.

"Are you trying to say something?"

"I don't know daddy, am I? Look me in my face and tell me you didn't do this." Looking straight at his daughter he was unable to utter the words. He hadn't done it, but he had hired someone to follow his wife. What he hadn't counted on was the investigator selling the photos to the tabloid. He had simply planned to use them as leverage with Malcolm. He knew how focused he was on protecting Cinnamon. He had found out about the cabin a couple years earlier after Malcolm had a heart attack. Last night he had told the investigator to watch his house and he had followed her to the cabin, snapping the photos. He sold the photos for five thousand dollars, not realizing those photos were worth twenty times that.

"Daddy, how could you? How would you feel if mama splashed those nasty pictures of you all over the newspaper?" He flinched at her words.

"She would never do that."

"No daddy, she wouldn't and you shouldn't have either. You know she's trying to start an educational center. Or was your intent to stop her!"

"No! I didn't even think of that." He confessed to her what he had done and why.

"Dad, you really need to grow-up. These kinds of underhanded tactics are going to insure that you lose her." Turning on her heel she slammed out of the door. Turning around, she reentered his office.

"Who is the investigator? He stared at her. "Dad!"

"Raoul Bennett." Nodding she walked from his office. *Damn!* Immediately the phone rang.

"William, this is Gladys Dubois. If you have lunch plans please cancel them. I want to see you at my house at one p.m. sharp."

"Yes ma'am." He wasn't sure if she heard him because he heard a dial tone in his ear. Real fear pierced his heart because he knew how much Cinnamon's family loved her and how powerful her aunt was, even in her eighties. She had financed his business when they had moved back to Center City years ago. He remembered that night he told her he was going to finance his business. She asked him how much it would cost. Without blinking an eye she had written him a check for a quarter million dollars, interest free. He was almost done paying her.

Walking into Gladys' house William could smell roasting beef and her signature macaroni and cheese. He gave her a kiss on the cheek before following her into the kitchen. He blinked when he saw the tabloid open on table. He watched her quietly fill their plates, humming, *Love don't love nodody.*' The last time he had felt this intimidated was when he asked Cinnamon's mom if he could marry her. After the plates were filled she sat down next to him. For several minutes they ate quietly. Finally she broke the silence.

"William, I love you like a son, but if you bring harm to my niece... I'll kill you." Shock entered his mind. He couldn't believe what he had heard.

"Ma'am?" He looked at her banana colored face, she looked completely calm.

"What I said is that I love you like a son, but if you bring harm to Cinnamon Dubois Brown I'll kill you. I'll shoot you in your cheating heart. Don't look so puzzled. I know you been 'slinging' it for years. Isn't that the current terminology? My niece chose to look the other way, so I let her. Her business is her business. I had to tell my sister that years ago or you would already be dead. But listen to me and listen good, if you try to drag her through the mud or hurt her you'll be sorry. I have no problem spending the rest of my years in the penitentiary. I'm almost eighty-three years old. I'm sure they will feel sorry and send me some place nice like they sent Martha Stewart." For several minutes he stared at her. "Now go on and eat your food, I know you love roast beef and macaroni and cheese. And don't worry I didn't poison it. I already told you how I will take you out." Without another word she went back to eating her food, talking about Amy, the weather and other such topics. When he prepared to leave, she placed a large packet of food in his hands, kissing him on the forehead. He felt like he had been kissed by the Mob.

****

Lord, that woman just told me to my face that she would kill me and I believe her. I never knew that everyone in town knew my business. I thought I was so discreet. Brown thought about the events of the day as he drove back to his office. He wondered why he hadn't heard from Malcolm Black or his wife.

Chapter Ten

Black watched Cinnamon walk into the Center. She nodded at him, walking back to her office. She smiled to let him know things were okay. For the remainder of the day they worked on plans for her new venture, never discussing anything except business. At five she looked up at him.

"Can we order dinner, I'm starving."

"Order dinner, are you going to eat here with me?"

"That's the plan. Then I'm going home to prepare Muha's room for tomorrow."

"What would you like?"

"Curried oxtails sound really good and I know Ms. Bertha will deliver to her favorite client."

"She will. However, I'm going to run around there to get them. It will only take a few minutes. Spread a table for us."

"Okay."

After they had eaten, Black asked Cinnamon if she had talked to Brown about the tabloid photos.

"No, I haven't, and I don't plan to, I hope you haven't said anything either."

"Not a word, though I know who took them. I talked Gabriel into telling me."

"I really don't want to know. I was shocked when I saw them, but after thinking about it, I realized I really don't care one way or the other. There could be any number of reasons why I was at your place and none of them are the business of anyone but us. My auntie and Aura understands, beyond that I'm not concerned."

"What about Muhammad?" A flicker of pain crossed Cinnamon's brow.

"I'm not sure. I haven't spoken to him in a few days, since I told him I wired him a ticket. Aura hasn't discussed it with him either and I don't know what Brown has done."

"You look concerned about it."

"I am a bit. Muhammad and I have always been really close, but on this I think he'll probably side with his daddy. He's…I don't know, we'll see." A touch of concern entered his mind. He knew how loyal her son was to both his parents. He was also worried how this would affect them. He chose to keep his concerns to himself, for now.

"So how long is Muhammad going to be here?"

"Just Friday night and Saturday morning, he's flying out on Saturday afternoon. He was supposed to stay until Sunday but he has plans."

"Will I see you this weekend?"

"Maybe on Sunday afternoon, I'm thinking about going to Sarasota next week. I need to get away. Can you come for a couple of days?"

"I would love that, let me know. Cinnamon as much as I love you, I'm truly sorry about all of this."

"I know you are." Standing up, she leaned over kissing him before leaving the Center.

Chapter Eleven

The next evening Muhammad and Brown arrived at the same time. Cinnamon was surprised to see he didn't have any luggage. He kissed her upon arrival, but there was something in his posture that concerned her. After sitting down, she told him exactly what she had told Aura. Brown sat quietly with a smug look on his face, not saying anything. Turning to his dad, Muhammad said, "Dad could you give mama and I some time alone?" Nodding, Brown stood up, walking from the house.

"Mama, why are you doing this now?"

"Doing what now?"

"Planning to leave Dad, you have known who he is for all the years you've been married. He has never been any different. Now, all of a sudden, you are ready to tear up a family. Mama I find that to be very selfish, considering." White hot pain poured through Cinnamon's veins at the words her son had spoken.

"Considering what, Muha?"

"Considering for the past couple of years you have been running around with Malcolm Black." An involuntary gasp escaped her throat.

"Is that what I was doing Muha, running around? Is that what you think I was doing? Just getting some from Malcolm, to tide me over through the lonely nights, while your dad was simply doing what he has always done? Is that it son?" The pain in her voice and on her face caused her son to squirm a bit.

"I'm not saying that, but I'm saying that back when I was a teenager and grandma was sick, he was always around you. Everyone could see how much he loved you. I heard grandma and granddaddy talking about it one time when I was over there."

"When my mother was sick, Malcolm was the best friend I had. Your dad was running around God knows where, you stayed in trouble at school, your sister wasn't talking to me and if it hadn't been for him I would have lost my damn mind. He never said a word to me about love, sex or nothing. He was just there for me. And not that it's your business, but you're a grown man, here it is. Malcolm and I did have a love affair for a couple of years, a love affair that included everything that love affairs include. But for almost two years all we have been is friends and business partners! That's it! Contrary to what you may think you know and may have heard that's the whole truth. And the reason I'm doing this now is because I have chosen to. I'm tired of being Mrs. Brown and looking the other way, while Mr. Brown gets to do anything he wants to. And if you don't like it Muhammad Dubois Brown, I really don't give a damn! And I certainly don't care what gossips have to say!" She leaned so close to his face he could smell the mint on her breath. He thought she might hit him.

"Mama, I didn't…"

"Get out of here and go tell your pitiful daddy that it didn't work!" Pushing back her chair, she slowly stood up, walking upstairs. Several minutes later she heard the door close.

****

"Dad, I messed up, I have never seen mama madder or more hurt." Brown sat across from his son in the hotel room he was staying in.

"I'm sorry son. I thought you would make an impact on her. The two of you were so close."

"I'm sure I messed that up. I'm going back over there to talk to her, but first I plan to talk to Black. Maybe I can talk some sense into him."

"Son, don't do that. It will probably make your mama madder. I have messed up this time, if only they hadn't taken those pictures."

"Pictures?" Brown realized he was talking out loud, he hadn't meant to say that to his son. "What pictures dad?"

"Someone took pictures of me and someone and sent them to your mama, trying to blackmail her for money."

"Dad, please tell me that's not true!" Unable to look at his son, Brown nodded his head.

"Dad, why in the world didn't you tell me that before I went over there insulting mama? Lord!

54

Look dad, I'm going by to talk to Black and then I'm going to see my sister!" *I guess I messed that up, I thought he could help.*

****

Black wasn't at all surprised when he saw Muhammad Brown get out of the rental car, pulling into his driveway. He was sitting on the porch, enjoying a bottle of beer. Standing up he grabbed the younger man into an embrace. He was pleased when he hugged him back.

"So how's the left coast?"

"It's all good. So what are your intentions where my mama is concerned?" Smiling slightly, the older man held the glance of the younger man.

"They're all honorable. When your mother divorces your father I plan to marry her. Muhammad, I mean no disrespect to your father or any of you but I love her. I have loved her for almost forty years. I did everything in my power to stay away from her but circumstances and life continually placed us together. And whether you believe it or not I'm sorry about all of this. I have never seen her in more pain, your dad either for that matter. But just as sure as she becomes free, I will marry her."

Nodding at his friend and mentor, Muhammad picked up the open bottle of beer, sipping from it. For almost an hour the two of them sat on the porch, swapping the beer between them, saying nothing. Finally, Muhammad stood up.

"I'm going to head out. Thanks for being honest with me. I just never thought my family would break up. Mama and dad are the only people I know who have been married so long. I thought they loved each other."

"Muhammad, they do love each other, but sometimes love isn't enough." The truth of that statement penetrated both their hearts.

"You understand that I have to support my dad."

"I totally understand that and it does nothing to change the love I have for you."

"Me either." Black watched the young man walk down the driveway, understanding that at twenty-four years of age, he was becoming a man. These kinds of situations caused growth, painful growth, but growth nonetheless.

Chapter Twelve

Sitting across the table from his sister, Muhammad told Aura what had transpired.

"Muha, you're going to have stay out of this. This is between mama and dad. And I'm sorry but in this case mama is totally justified. That woman's husband took mama, butt naked, sexual pictures of dad with his wife." Muhammad shuddered at the thought of how his mom must have felt. Getting up Aura went to retrieve, *'Black News, To Use,'* throwing a copy to her brother. Shock marred his face at the picture on the cover.

"Please tell me dad wasn't behind this."

"I'm afraid so. According to dad, he hired Raoul Bennett to 'keep an eye' on Mama. Mr. Bennett took it upon himself to follow her the other night. He then sold them to Gabriel for five thousand dollars and he put them in that rag."

"Five thousand dollars...! Do you mean to tell me that fool had photos like that involving a woman worth a few million and a man worth tens of millions and he sold them for five thousand dollars. What an idiot!"

"Umm hmm. No one really knows what mama is worth. Actually, my guess is that Gabriel had an ax to grind with mama. After she started writing for **Black Venue** he asked her to write for him. Of course she turned him down; she didn't want to be a part of that trash. When he saw how big the magazine got based on mama's articles alone he has held a grudge ever since. The good news is that most people know it is garbage. I made Raoul give me all the film he had taken."

"How much did that cost you?"

"Not a penny. I know him. He forgot I was mama's daughter. When I showed up he knew it was over. I referred him to an attorney friend a year ago who literally saved him from prison. He knows I'm not the one!" Smiling at his sister, Muhammad swallowed down a lump.

"Do you think mama will forgive me?"

"Of course she will. We can go over there in the morning to take her to breakfast."

"She said damn, twice. I thought she was going to hit me, but the hardest thing was seeing all that pain on her face. Do you really think she'll divorce him?"

"I do, I didn't at first. But number one, mama has never said the word divorce before. Number two, she has never had visual evidence like that and Muha it was very visual. The other day I was at the house and was snooping and found them. They are very graphic. And this newspaper thing is probably the deal sealer."

"Not, only that but there is the Black factor."

"There is that. Mama loves him Muhammad and he sure enough loves him some Ms. Cinnamon. I hate to admit this but he's better suited for mama. I haven't seen him with a woman other than mama or family members in years and I see him all the time. We attend many of the same functions. He's a rich, handsome man and he could have his pick of women and he only has eyes for Cinnamon Bun. He treats her like the Queen she is. That's titanic."

"It is. Do you think dad will marry again, if mama marries?"

"I don't know. I don't think daddy will stay in Center City, if they get married. I think he's more worried about that than anything. Daddy has a lot of pride, if mama marries Black he'll move from town."

"What a mess. I didn't know dad was out there like that."

"He always has been Muha. I can remember when I was a little girl and we were living in Miami and Los Angeles. Mama would be so sad-faced sometimes. Dad is like a lot of old school brothers. They feel that so long as they pay the bills, buy gifts and take care of home, it's okay to have a little bit on the side. I don't know, but I guess mama looked away many times. I wasn't at all surprised when she got involved with Black, I thought she would leave daddy then."

"Yeah, look sis, I'm going to take a nap. Let's go see mama tomorrow morning. I need to fix things with her before I head out."

"Okay. How are the marriage plans?"

59

"They're on hold. I was going to tell mama this week anyway. It seems like I'm more like my dad than I want to admit."

Chapter Thirteen

Cinnamon stood in her backyard staring at the waterfall. After a restless night she had gotten up at five a.m. In the past couple of hours she had worked on her business plan for the Empowerment Place, watered her plants and consumed three cups of espresso. The words her son said to her had run through her mind all night. She understood his pain; the one thing her children had always been able to count on was her consistency. She had never dropped the ball on them. What they had to understand was that at almost thirty and twenty-four, their lives were their lives and hers was hers. She knew Aura understood. She'd had enough personal pain in the past couple of years of her own. Muhammad was still living in the circle of family love and hadn't had his head butted enough times. Even knowing that, his words had cut her to the bone. Turning to walk inside she was startled when she bumped into her son. He immediately picked her up, swinging her around the way he had done since becoming a teenager. Involuntary laughter poured from her. When he finally put her down, she looked into his dark brown face, which was so much like his father's.

"Are you here to be mean, if you are then leave..." Winking at her he pulled her down to the stone bench beneath the huge oak trees that covered the property.

"No, ma'am, I come in peace. Mama, I'm sorry. I didn't know. I just saw how hurt dad was and I wanted to do something. Mama, I hate to see you guys break up. Yours is the only marriage I know that works."

"Muhammad, one of the things I tried to teach my children is not to run off half-cocked. You came into battle with me yesterday, completely unarmed. I would have appreciated it if you had simply asked me, allowing me a voice. I also understand why your father came to you. He knew Aura's feelings, his dad thinks he's a fool and Aunt Gladys threatened to put a bullet in his heart, he needed and wanted an advocate. What you and your father have to understand is that I simply am not willing to look the other way any longer. We have both made mistakes, the biggest mistake I made in my marriage is allowing my husband to feel he can do whatever he wants to do and that I will always wrap my arms around his mess. Son, I have been doing that all my life. Even with you children. When Aura decided not to talk to me for years, I chased her down. When you were in ninth and tenth grades and decided that mediocre grades and weed smoke was all you needed, I stood in there, keeping secrets and making it all better. I am tired of that, all I want is to love God and live however many years I have left in a loving and respectful situation. I know your daddy loves me but he doesn't respect me and I can no longer accept that." Muha nodded with tears in his eyes.

"Aura is coming in a little bit with Amy. We're going to cook you breakfast and hang out with you. Dad is picking me up at eleven to take me to the airport. So go soak in bubbles and we will get this show on the road.

After her children left Cinnamon sat quietly in her big, empty home. When she and Brown moved back to Florida they had decided to remodel the house her parents had lived in. Her father had died when Cinnamon was a young girl and her mother had moved back to the family homestead. This house had sat empty for years surrounded by lakes, vegetation and wildlife. She had modernized it and added seven hundred square feet to it when she and Brown returned home. For years it had been filled with family, friends and laughter. For the past few weeks it had been a big, lonely house. Muhammad was in Los Angeles, Aura and Amy lived across town in one of the new condos and Brown was in a hotel room in town. She wasn't sure yet but she was thinking about moving. She had her mom's house near her aunt and this house.

Chapter Fourteen

*I had a different sermon for this morning, but I
have decided to focus on the sanctity of marriage.
God put it on my heart this morning to address how
lightly some take their wedding vows. It seems like
in this day and age of overnight divorces a woman
feels she can get up and discard a husband, a
family, like so much tissue paper. Church, I want
someone to tell me what happened to love, forgiving
and longsuffering. Somebody has to say that pride
goes before a fall.*

Sitting in the early service, Cinnamon felt Pastor
Walker's word rain down on her head like boiling
water. She had witnessed so many sermons where
he had used the pulpit as a place to call out
members of his congregation. She knew it was now
her turn. His words continued to flow around her
head and resonate in her heart. She also knew it
didn't matter what he said. Only God would be her
judge. Knowing that didn't stop her from feeling
pained. After the service she hurried to her car.
She was planning to meet Malcolm for dinner, but
she really needed to go home.

****

Arriving at her doorstep, she retrieved the
newspaper lying in the doorway. Pulling it from the
plastic sleeve, she gasped when she saw an almost
identical picture of the one in **Black News To Use,**
except this time the woman's face was clearly
visible and it wasn't her. It was Delia, Black's
sister. It was astonishing how similar the pictures
were down to the clothing, complete with the black

dress and the silky white shawl. Getting up and walking to the den, she pulled out the older newspaper and the resemblance was uncanny, considering she and Delia were the same size and the other photo only showed her from the rear. The caption below the picture read, *'a photo is worth a thousand words.'* Uninhibited laughter poured from her throat and she immediately felt better. She knew exactly what had occurred. Black had made sure someone took a picture of him and his sister, simulating the other photo. It was pure genius and love in its purest form. Before she could dial him, the phone rang. Looking at the caller-id she saw the name of her daughter.

"Hello."

"Cinnamon Bun, please tell me how you did that. Ms. Delia looks just like you in that photo. She even has on your clothes."

"I didn't do it."

"Uh, I should have known, this has Malcolm Black written all over it."

"Only he could think of something like that. I was about to call him."

"He didn't ask you first?"

"No, I would have told him not to bother. But it's really lovely."

"It sure is. What are you cooking, me and Amy are starving?"

"I roasted a chicken, but I'm meeting Malcolm for lunch. I will drop it off to you; I'm meeting him at the Center."

"Thanks mama. See you in a bit."

Cinnamon ran upstairs changing into a bright yellow sundress, draping to the floor. She had been wearing somber colors for weeks. It was time to shake that off. After changing she filled a picnic basket with the chicken and other food for her girls.

****

Walking into her daughter's home Cinnamon was always pleased by the mix of the old and the new. There were many pieces she had given Aura that had belonged to her and her mother. Otherwise, the place with filled with modern African pieces and the beautiful art of unknown and famous African-American artists. Immediately she picked up Amy and started nibbling on her neck. Aura watched indulgently from the floor. After she was exhausted, Cinnamon and the baby plopped down beside Aura.

"Well, lady you look mighty fetching in all that yellow. It's nice to see you looking like a breath of fresh air."

"Thank you. I feel okay. Did you watch the nine o'clock service?"

"I did, I wasn't going to mention it to you. The camera panned to your face when he was talking."

66

"Oh lord, did it show how pained I was?"

"Only to those who know you, have you spoken to him?"

"No, I'm actually going to make a point to go by there tomorrow."

"Have you spoken to daddy?"

"Not since yesterday. Is he okay?"

"He's fine. I think he's mad at me though. He wanted me to see about getting him an apartment near here and I told him no. I need my privacy. I hope he didn't take it wrong. I just don't want daddy popping in on me all the time."

"Don't feel bad. I'm thinking about moving myself. Do you and Amy want to move into the house?" Aura tried to hide the shock on her face, but failed. For the first time it felt real that her parents were separated.

"Where would you move to, Grandma's house?"

"I don't know. I know that I'm not going to stay in that big old house alone. I can't sell it because it's on family land. Actually, I'm not going to move in mama's house either. Too many memories and it's too close to Aunt Gladys. I feel a need for privacy also. I am thinking about moving closer to the coast. I would love a small place on the beach."

"You're thinking about leaving Center City?"

"I guess so, though it's only about forty miles to the ocean. I'm not making any hasty decisions though. I plan to take my time about all of this. Baby, I need to go now."

"Okay, when does Alexandra get back?"

"She's due back next week. She was supposed to be gone only two weeks but extended her time."

"Does she know?"

"No, she doesn't and I didn't want to bother her. She's still recovering from Glen's marriage and I knew if I told her she would have rushed back."

"Maybe you need to get away."

"I do. I'm going to Sarasota next week. I'm in need of a vacation." Standing up the women walked to the door. Aura held her mother tightly, sniffing her signature Addict perfume by Christian Dior.

Chapter Fifteen

Black had decorated the library at the Center to look like a small café. There was a round table with a white linen tablecloth. The table was set with roses and real crystal. The air was filled with music and the fragrance of fine foods. He was staring out the window. He looked so handsome dressed in all black clothing. His eyes filled with the sight of his love. He pulled her into his arms the minute she walked in, holding her close to his heart.

"Hey Black Man, this is very lovely. Thank you."

"There is never any need to thank me. I'll do anything for you." Pulling away, she walked over lifting the covers from the plates. She was pleased to see soft shell crabs and lobster salad.

"That's obvious. What made you think of having that photo of you and Delia done?"

"I knew I needed to do something. I couldn't rest. I bought you that shawl, and I knew that dress came from L. Minton's boutique so that was easy. You and Delia are the same size, except she has no booty. I hope the new picture didn't show her from the back. That would have been a dead giveaway. What helped was the first picture was so grainy that things like complexion and hair weren't an issue. I would do anything for you."

"I know."

"What does Brown think?" Black pulled out a chair, allowing Cinnamon to sit down. He sat next to her.

"I don't know. The only time I have spoken to him in the last few days was with Muha. He has been sending me daily text messages. I think he's worried I'm going to ask him about the photos. Did you see Pastor Walker's sermon this morning?"

"Yeah, I saw it. I also saw your face. Did that feel personal to you?"

"It did. He and Brown are good friends and he has always used the pulpit to make points. But it's cool. I plan to talk to him tomorrow and to Brown. I have filed for a legal separation."

"A legal separation and then what?"

"And then a divorce at some point, I'm taking my time. Brown and I have a lot of joint assets and the house which I owned has been greatly contributed to by him. I may have to buy him out."

"Cinnamon, will you ever marry me?" Looking straight into his dark eyes, she wanted him to see her heart.

"Are you proposing to me?"

"Maybe…"

"Then the answer is yes I will, but, I need some time. That is why I'm getting a legal separation.

That way you and I will be able to date. You can court me." Pleasure lit his eyes at her words.

"For real…"

"For real, now let's eat this lovely food and then I want us to hug and kiss and... Are you sure there are no cameras in here." Giggles erupted from both of them.

Chapter Sixteen

"Hey." Looking up from her magazine Cinnamon was startled to see her husband standing next to her lounge chair. He had always walked softly. He was very handsome in a dark tan suit, with shirt opened at the throat. Her heart turned over at the pain in his face. He had always looked younger than his years but today he looked all of his fifty-four years.

"Hey you...come on sit down." He sat down across from her.

"Pastor Walker told me you came to see him a few days ago."

"I did, I wanted him to hear my side of the story."

"Did he tell you that he wanted us to try counseling?"

"He did, but Brown I don't want to go to counseling. I want a legal separation. I want to be on my own for a while."

"On your own, does that mean you won't be getting remarried immediately?"

"Brown, I'm still married to you, for the time being. However, if I decide to remarry, I will do you the courtesy of telling you." He was embarrassed by the tears that surfaced in his eyes. The fact that he was in pain hurt her. She loved

Brown and didn't want him in pain. She was just unable to stay married to him.

"B, I'm sorry that things are the way they are. I'm sorry I made you feel it was okay to be with other women. I'm sorry I love Malcolm and I'm most sorry you are in pain."

"I know you are. Cinnamon I love you, more than anything and I can't imagine my life without you. I don't know why I..."

"Brown, maybe you should go to counseling. That might help you deal with all of this. I would advise it be someone other than Pastor Walker. Sometimes we need an unbiased ear."

"I might do that. By the way I have an apartment downtown, one of the lofts over the bank. What do you plan to do about the house?"

"I don't know, it was too big for us, it's certainly too big for me. I want to be near the ocean. I asked Aura if she wanted to move in with the baby. She didn't answer me. We'll see. Would you like some dinner?" His eyes lit up at her words.

"I would love that. Are you going to eat with me?"

"Yes, Brown I don't hate you, I'm no longer even mad with you. We've had a wonderful life together but it's time for changes." She walked inside to prepare plates for the two of them. Walking back outside, she sat down to share a meal with her husband, the father of her children and hopefully someone who would always be a part of her life.

****

Driving into town Brown couldn't deal with the pain he felt and the rage in his heart, against himself. He had spent two hours with his wife, she had treated him the way she always had, but everything told him she had moved on, turned a corner. The idea of never holding her in his arms or making love to her was more than he could bear.

****

I'm so sorry to see Brown in so much pain, but I have moved on. I love him but I can no longer be his wife. I have spent so many years sucking down feelings and trying to lessen who I am, to be with him. What I know for sure is that Brown is Brown and no matter what he will always be who he is. It's time for me to find out who I am.

****

Cinnamon packed her suitcase, preparing to get on the road to Sarasota the next morning. She was going to spend a couple of days alone and Black was going to come down to spend a couple of days with her.

Chapter Seventeen

After two days of complete rest Cinnamon felt restored. For two and a half days she had slept late, taken long walks along the beach and read for pleasure. She hadn't spoken to anyone from home. She had informed Aura, Aunt Gladys and Muha not to contact her unless it was an emergency. She had owned the cabin on a deserted part of Sarasota beach for many years. She had gone there through the years with her mother, her children, Alexandra and a few times with Black. He was due any minute now. She hadn't spoken to him but she was sure he was on his way.

****

Preparing to leave the Learning Center Black was surprised to see Brown walking in.

"Hey man, what's up?"

"Not much, how about you?"

"I'm good...I was about to take off, is something going on?"

"Other than the fact that I'm almost legally separated from my wife, and my life is going up in smoke, I'm cool." Brown sat down at the table, forcing Black to sit down next to him.

"So where are you going?" Black looked at Brown without answering. "Don't say anything. I know you are going to be with my wife. She has been missing in action the past couple of days. I don't blame you. So once you marry her, will I get invited over for Christmas and holidays the way I allowed you in?" Black remained silent, he totally understood the pain Brown was in and he allowed him to vent.

"You and she are just alike, so quiet and cold. Anyway tell her I love her..." Standing up, Brown walked out before he did or said something he couldn't take back. The papers for the legal separation had shown up on his desk yesterday. He wasn't sure he was going to sign them. It felt too final to him. He had gone by the house and Cinnamon hadn't answered. He had even asked Aura, Muhammad and Aunt Gladys and they had all refused to say. His instincts told him that Black was going to see her. He knew he was going to follow him.

Pulling away from the Center, Black checked his rear view mirror. He suspected Brown was going to follow him. He called Cinnamon to tell her he had a delay. He was going to call Brown's bluff. Instead of driving to Sarasota he drove to the outskirts of town pulling into the parking lot of the Hilton. He went in as if to check in. Once inside he called his driver to bring another car to him. After thirty minutes he walked through the back gate getting into the car his driver had brought for him. Driving away he saw Brown's truck parked next to his car. He had instructed his driver to wait an additional thirty minutes before moving the vehicle.

Brown was shocked when he saw Black's limo driver walk to the car, pulling out. Immediately he knew he had wasted an hour sitting there waiting for Cinnamon to show up. It was just as well, he wasn't sure what he would have done if she had shown up. It seemed Black always was one step ahead of everyone. What he had done with the newspaper had been pure genius. Maybe Cinnamon was right, he did need therapy.

****

"So what caused the delay?" Black was sitting on the chaise lounge on the balcony looking out over the ocean with Cinnamon. He pondered whether he should tell her and decided to.

"I don't know what to say. I thought Brown was dealing with this. We had dinner the other night and he seemed okay."

"Cinnamon, he isn't going to deal with this. He loves you. I think he received the separation papers. There was a desperate air about him. I felt his pain."

"Would you have done what he did?"

"Most definitely, there have been many times over the years when I showed up at places only because I knew you were going to be there. I simply wanted to be around you. And I'm telling you the truth, if you left me now, I would be a stalking fool. Brown is handling it better than I would. I would be a menace."

"Really, I can't imagine..."

"That's because you're you. Most women would have done major damage to Brown by now. That classy thing you do is rare. I remember when you confronted him in Atlanta. Most sisters would have karate kicked him and beat the woman down."

"I have karate kicked Brown a couple of times, but never in public. And the woman owes me nothing, that isn't my way."

"Maybe if it had been you wouldn't be going through this now."

"I also wouldn't be sitting here with you, sipping mojitos and planning to jump your bones in a few minutes..." Winking at her he stood up walking inside.

"In that case, I'm so glad you're a classy lady." Draining her glass, Cinnamon stood, following him inside.

Chapter Eighteen

For two weeks after returning from Sarasota
Cinnamon was caught in a whirlwind of activity.
The city government had approved her request to
open the Empowerment Place. It was considered a
tutoring center. She couldn't actually teach but she
could assist with homework and tutor. Mostly what
she wanted it to be was a place where emerging
women between the ages of twelve and eighteen
could come for fun and acceptance. During the
school months her plan was to be open from two
until six p.m. During the summer months she would
be open from eight a.m. until four p.m. She had
space for twenty girls. To assist her she had two
fulltime tutors and three tutors on call. She was
very excited about it. It was going to be a wide
open space filled with books, a piano, jukebox, a
large dance floor and a kitchen. Most, importantly,
she was pleased with financing it herself. The
money she had received from book sales would get
it started and running for three years. After that she
would tap into some of her inheritance. She hadn't
seen Brown since returning, nor had she heard from
him. She had seen Amy and Aura most days and
Aunt Gladys a couple of times. She was going to
see them all later that evening. Aura was being
honored by the local bar association for having one
of the fastest growing law offices in Central Florida.
Cinnamon knew Brown would be there and Black
had told her that Aura invited him. Muhammad
wasn't going to be able to make it. Cinnamon
suspected he wanted to stay out of the fray.

Cinnamon arrived at the fete right on time. Black was already in attendance, his sister Delia was with him. Cinnamon was sitting at the head table with Aura. Approximately ten minutes after arriving Brown walked in with a young woman on his arm. She appeared to be about thirty and was very lovely and dressed provocatively in a low-cut black dress. Cinnamon was surprised that she didn't feel a bit of pain. Brown was especially handsome in a dark blue suit. He walked to her table with the young woman.

"Hello Cinnamon, are these seats reserved?"

"Hi William, they are for you and I and I assume your date."

"Oh yeah, Cinnamon this is Andrea Wills, she is my new office manager. Andrea this is my estranged wife, Cinnamon Dubois Brown."

"Oh my God, I know who you are. You wrote that book, *'So What if I Love Them Both?'* I loved that book. You have the most unique voice. If I had known you were here I would've bought my book for you to sign. Oh my God!" Cinnamon smiled indulgently, while Brown appeared uncomfortable. "So Mrs. Brown, are you writing a new book and what will it be called?"

"I'm writing a few things, but I think I will do a sequel entitled, *'So What if I Left One of Them?'*"

"Oh my God, that would be so awesome!" Peals of laughter flew from Cinnamon's throat at the sour look on Brown's face. Aura walked over to the table at the sound of her mother's laughter.

"Hey mama, hey dad, Andrea what are you doing here?"

"This is your dad? Oh my God, I didn't even know. We went to school together. I didn't even know. I have been moving around here and there. I decided to come home and your dad hired me."

"To do what, last I heard you were an underwear model?" Cinnamon cracked up again at the dry tone in her daughter's voice. She was too tickled.

"Oh no! I just got my real estate license. I needed to move home, California got to be too expensive." Brown sat down and couldn't stop staring at his wife. She looked absolutely beautiful in a creamy brown, floor length dress with three-quarter length sleeves. Her hair was glossy and her makeup understated. She had yellow diamond earrings in her ears and a three carat yellow diamond ring on her right hand. He was pleased to see she still had on her wedding band. His eyes flickered towards Black who nodded at him.

"Mama, where is Aunt Gladys, I thought you were bringing her?"

"I was but she's coming with a man, there she is now. Where's the baby?"

"I decided to leave her with the sitter. She has been a little cranky today and I didn't want her in here showing out. You know how that little diva can be. Daddy this table was for you, mama and Aunt Gladys. Since you have a date and Aunt Gladys has a date, I'm going to ask you to move to the other table." Walking over to the table behind them, she pointed for Black and Delia to join her mother. Leaning towards Cinnamon, Black asked if it were okay.

"Absolutely..." Brown realized his ploy to embarrass Cinnamon had backfired. He was the one with egg on his face. All of a sudden Andrea's chatter was getting on his nerves. She couldn't stop talking about how beautiful Cinnamon was and how much she loved her books. He saw Black pick up Cinnamon's right hand, looking at the ring, smiling into her eyes. It took everything in him not to get up and walk out. Looking around he was glad most of the people in attendance were younger people who didn't know him.

The ceremony was beautiful and Brown and Cinnamon couldn't have been prouder. Aura was the toast of Center City. In her speech she had thanked her dad for spoiling her, her mother for loving her unconditionally and Malcolm Black for throwing so much business her way she could barely keep up. For a couple of hours after the ceremony there had been dinner, dancing and drinks. After seeing Black and Cinnamon dance Brown had left with Andrea in tow.

"So Cinnamon how did it feel seeing Brown with that woman?" The two of them were sitting near the duck pond, outside the auditorium where the ceremony was held.

"I didn't feel anything. The whole thing was so funny. Did you hear her carrying on about my books? Of all the women he could have invited he had to go and get a Cinnamon Dubois Brown groupie. And not only that, but she went to school with Aura. That child must have said, 'Oh my God,' fifty times. Too funny..."

"You look so beautiful and thanks for wearing that ring and those earrings."

"Why wouldn't I wear them, I got 'em from my man." Smiling at her words, he wrapped his arms around her. They sat on the bench watching the ducks until 2 a.m.

Chapter Nineteen

Black sat across the desk from one of his attorneys. Aura Brown handled his school business, but Dennis Rogers, his frat brother, handled most other things.

"Write him a check."

"Say what?" Dennis thought he had misunderstood.

"I say write him a check. If he wants to sue me for a million dollars for alienation of affection, write him a check." Brown had brought a lawsuit against Malcolm Black accusing him of alienation of affection from his wife, Cinnamon Dubois Brown. Black knew he was lashing out in pain.

"Man are you crazy, you are simply going to hand that man one million dollars in hard, cold, cash, no questions asked?"

"Sure, if that's what he wants. Just draft up something, make him sign it saying he won't bring any more frivolous lawsuits and give him a check. There is nothing to contest. He could have asked for more, I would have given it to him."

"Damn! Is she worth all that?"

"She is worth everything I own and all I can beg, borrow or steal. He doesn't want my money, he wants to hurt me. I understand that. He feels the same way I felt thirty-three years ago when he betrayed me. I told him I planned to come home

84

and marry her. A year later I get there and they are walking down the aisle. I get what's up. Give it to him."

"Man, I thought ya'll were boys, he is our frat and all. We all vowed to never let a woman come between us. I really hate to see this. Not only that but man they have been married a long time." A shimmer of pain crossed Black's brow.

"I know. Dennis, I did everything I could to stay away from Cinnamon. For years I avoided her. When they moved back here, he befriended me. When her mother was ill we got real close. He was neglecting her and I took care of her. Man, I just wanted to be around her. I never put my hands on her. For years he took that woman for granted, creeping here and sleeping there. She forgave him over and over. This last time she'd had enough. I told him for years that if she left him I would be there. There's no way in hell, I'm going to let her be free and not be with her. I'm not a saint."

"I feel you. I tell you one thing. I don't want to love nothing like that. Brown has always been out there. I often wondered if she knew. She's so damn fine and pretty, though a little cold for my tastes. So I figured he had his reasons. But man, he loves that woman."

"He does, and so do I. Write him a check."

85

Three days later Brown showed up on Black's doorstep. Black opened the door, letting him in. He threw the check on the coffee table.

"So did you tell her?"

"Tell who?"

"My wife... who else?"

"Man, you know I don't work like that. Dennis told me you sued me, I told him to pay you."

"Black... man why you got to do this? There are millions of women out there, why do you have to have her?"

"For the same reasons you had to have her. There's no one like her. I have had women and more women. There's only one Cinnamon. Brown you did this, I didn't. What did you think I was going to do, fight you over a million dollars?"

"I don't know what I thought...I don't know...anything anymore. Man I want my wife, please don't do this."

"I don't know what to say man."

"Say, you won't marry her."

"I can't say that." Brown pushed hard into Black's chest, Black stumbled, almost falling to the floor. Shock arose in his heart. Grabbing Brown by his throat it took everything in him not to choke him. He pushed him forcefully away from him.

"Man, go home. I don't want to do this. I'm not going to fight you. Don't you ever touch me again! You really need to get a grip on yourself." Not saying a word Brown walked out.

Chapter Twenty

Cinnamon was lying on the floor reading to Amy. Aura had gone on an overnight trip and to Cinnamon's delight she had left Amy with her. The ringing doorbell interrupted them.

"Ring nanny."

"I know busy boo, let's see who it is." Looking out the glass pane, Cinnamon saw her best friend of over forty years standing there. Alexandra Wilson was back! Amy started jumping up and down.

"Annie Xan, Annie Xan!" They both flew into Alexandra's arms. She was bowled over with the reception. Alexandra was over six feet tall and an almond colored buff sister. She and Cinnamon had been best friends since first grade.

"Whoa, this is some reception. I knew I missed my people but this is nice. And look at my baby, Amy boo, you have grown so big, my goodness!"

"I big like nanny." Placing the baby on the floor Alexandra looked at Cinnamon. Her friend looked lovely but instinct told her something was wrong.

"Where's Brown?"

"Papoo gone, Nanny sad."

"Shhh. Come in and sit down. Amy, do you want to watch Sponge Bob?"

After getting Amy situated in the den, Cinnamon filled her best friend in on what had occurred in her life. For over an hour Alexandra listened in shock.

"Girl, why didn't you call me? I would have come home. Lord, what in the world was Brown thinking?"

"I didn't want to bother you. You had your own stuff to deal with. Isn't that something, both of us married over thirty years and getting divorced?"

"Yes it is, but I never thought you and Brown would divorce. How's Black?"

"He's fine. I think he feels guilty and he's worried I won't marry him."

"Should he be?"

"No. But I need some time. I'm legally separated from Brown. Once we work out all this property mess, I'm going to file for divorce. I would like Black to give me at least a year."

"I don't know my sister. That man has been waiting for over thirty years. He isn't going to like that. What do you want to do, play the field?"

"Girl no… are you crazy? Actually, I would like to be alone for awhile. I would love to be courted by Malcolm and sin with him a little bit, but I want to be Cinnamon Dubois for a little while. I want to sleep all night in my bed alone. Just for a little while." Cinnamon walked into the den to check on Amy. She was fast asleep with her thumb in her mouth. Cinnamon covered her with a cotton comforter. Walking over to the refrigerator, she retrieved a pint of Ben and Jerry's Cherry Garcia and two spoons. One of she and Alexandra's favorite things was eating an entire pint together.

"So when did you get back?"

"This morning, I'm so tired but I wanted to see a friendly face. How are the kids doing with this?"

"As you know, Aura is a cool as she could be. I wish you had been here to see her awards ceremony. Center City is in love with her."

"What about Muha?"

"He was a bit testy with me at first. But he's fine. I talk to him every few days. He has called his wedding off. I hope…"

"Cinnamon, don't worry about that boy. He'll be fine. Can I stay here with you and Lady Amy?"

"Please do." The phone rang.

"Hello."

"Are you okay?" Black.

"Yes, I'm fine, what about you?"

"I'm good. Cinnamon I love you. I never meant for this to happen between you and Brown, but I love you."

"Malcolm, I know that. Are you sure you're okay? Alexandra is here, but if you need me…" His heart quieted down at her words.

"No, that's okay. I just wanted to make sure you were okay and to tell you I love you."

"I'm fine and I love you too. Why don't you join us for breakfast in the morning?"

"I would love to eat breakfast with the three of you, but I don't want to come to…well, out there."

"Okay, so meet us at mama's house at eleven, we'll have brunch."

"Alright."

Chapter Twenty-One

The next morning after they had eaten brunch, Alexandra took Amy shopping so Black and Cinnamon could have some time alone. They were sitting on her mother's glassed in porch. Cinnamon could see Black was troubled.

"What's up, Black Man?

"Cinnamon, I can't go through all of this for you to decide to go back to Brown. That would kill me."

"Where is this coming from, I'm not going back to anyone. What I want to do is pray, spend sometime with Amy, you and get my center up and running. We're already legally separated. Once we have gotten our finances untangled, I plan to file for divorce. Then I need a breathing period."

"How long of a breathing period..."

"Probably a year..."

"A year, what the hell do you need a year for, do you plan to date?" Laughter spilled from Cinnamon, she stopped giggling at the serious look on Black's face.

"No, Negro, I don't plan to date. I have been married since I was twenty-one years old. What I want to do is sleep alone a few nights while eating cookies in bed. I want you to pick me up and take me out to dinner, the theatre, the opera and stuff like that. Then I want you to spend the night with me and I want to spend the night with you, sinning a little bit. Then, after the courtship I want you to propose to me so I can say yes. Then I want to run off to Jamaica and marry you with Aura giving me away and Alexandra as my best woman and Lady Amy as my flower girl…" Joy filled his heart at those words.

"Oh…

"Oh what? Something has happened, come on 'fess up."

"Well, Brown is tripping. First he tried to sue me, when I gave him a check, he came over last night and he was very confrontational. It could have gotten very ugly…thank God it didn't."

"He did what, what do you mean sue you?"

"He sued me for alienation of your affections."

"How much did he ask for?"

"A million…"

"What a louse, you are worth twenty times that and he asks for one measly million. Please." She burst out, howling with laughter. He had to join her. It was absurd when he thought about it.

"So you gave him the check?"

"Yeah, I would give him anything he wanted."

"I'm not for sale…"

"I wasn't trying to buy you, I was…I don't know what I was thinking. Dennis thought I was crazy."

"Dennis doesn't think any woman is worth that."

"Are you mad?"

"No, it's kind of cute. Though I know I'm worth more than that."

"You are, just like I told Dennis you are worth every dime I have and all I can beg, borrow and steal. I don't know if I can wait a year."

"You have waited for years!"

"I know… that's what scares me. Every time I think you belong to me something happens. I can't go through that again, I'm getting too old."

"You won't have to, just bear with me. We'll jump the broom. Maybe not jump it, but we'll skip it or something."

"Do you have time for us to go inside?"

"You're getting real greedy, for almost two years you're celibate. Now for the past few weeks every time I look around you're trying to wrap yourself around me."

"You said you wanted to do a little sinning. I want to help you with that." The two of them giggled like teenagers.

"No, we can't risk having anyone come over here. Aunt Gladys knows we're here and Amy has probably emptied Alexandra's pockets. So why don't we go to the cabin later. Aura is going to pick Amy up about five. I'll have her drop me off. You can bring me home tomorrow."

"Are you sure about that?"

"Umm hmm." He leaned over nibbling on her ear.

"Go home, save your nibbles, you're going to need them..."

Chapter Twenty-Two

"Daddy what do you think about me moving into the house? Mama suggested it, it would be nice for me and Amy and I love the country." Rubbing his eyes, Brown thought about what his daughter was saying and what it meant. They were eating lunch together at the Soul Café.

"It doesn't matter. Your mama told me she was thinking about moving. It had been too big for years. When Muha moved it really got big. I suppose it's too much for her. Do you know where she's moving?"

"She mentioned wanting to move near the ocean. It's about forty miles outside of town."

"What about her new venture?"

"Actually that would be closer for her. The tutoring center is about half way between town and where she wants to move."

"How is she?"

"She's fine daddy, this has all been hard for her. She loves you daddy and no one believes in marriage more than mama. But those photos..."

"I know. A couple of years ago Khadijah threatened to sue me and your mama handled her so beautifully. At that time she told me that if she ever had to deal with any more of my messes she would leave me. I didn't believe her. I know I have messed up over and over again, but we were a great team. We accomplished so much together. She hurt my feelings so bad the other day."

"How daddy?"

"She offered me a check for all the work I did on the house, our home. If she had spit in my face it couldn't have hurt me more."

"I'm sure she wasn't trying to do that. It's just that because she owns the property and it is heir property, she doesn't want to sell it and she probably figured you deserved something out of it. You guys lived there when you first got married and in the past decade you have poured a lot of money into it."

"I don't want money, I want my wife. Last night I saw her and Black sitting down on the square listening to jazz. She looked so beautiful and he looked so happy. He saw me, she didn't. Nothing ever felt so painful to me. I miss her so much, the way she smells, the way she laughs from deep down in her belly, even the way she cusses like a sailor when she's mad. The idea of never having any of that again is so hard for me. At first it was just my pride, now it's simply that I love and miss my wife. And Aura she will always be my wife." The pain in her father's voice brought a lump to her throat.

"What are you going to do when the divorce is final?"

"I'm thinking about moving to Tampa. It is close enough so I can see you and the baby and can come back to check on mom and dad. But it's far enough away that I won't have to run into Mr. and Mrs. Black all over town. You know what's funny I miss him, also. I never had a better friend than him. He was always honest about his feelings and I forced them together. I always knew he loved her. After he confessed his feelings for her, I figured I should keep my friend close and my enemies closer. I just didn't count on her falling in love with him. The three of us had great times together." For several minutes they sat in silence. Brown was the first person who saw Cinnamon walk into the restaurant. His eyes were filled with her. She was wearing a royal blue suit, with navy sling-back pumps. She didn't have on pantyhose or makeup other than lip-gloss. Her skin was glowing. Aura watched her dad watching her mom. *Why in the world couldn't he have been faithful to her?* Spotting them, Cinnamon walked over to join them with a huge smile on her face. She kissed Aura's face and kissed Brown on his head. Shocks of pleasure and desire ran through him like lava.

"Hey Browns what's up?" She plopped down in the chair between them. Immediately the waiter showed up with a glass of limeade. Brown smiled at that, everyone in Center City knew her. Glancing at her, he was unable to speak, sensing that, Aura decided to make conversation.

"So Cinnamon Bun, what has you all aglow this afternoon?"

"They have started remodeling my building. I was going to open the EP in the fall, but it looks like I'll be able to get in right after Labor Day. That is only a bit better than two months away. I'm so excited. Me, and mama used to talk about that years ago."

"Your mama would be very proud of this and you." Brown had found his voice, though it sounded funny to his own ears. Smiling at him, Cinnamon nodded.

"B, I know she would be. This was a dream of ours. How are you?"

"I'm hanging in there, you look beautiful."

"Thank you." After several minutes Brown decided to make his departure. Impulsively, he leaned over, kissing his wife on the cheek. He was very pleased that she simply smiled at him, winking. The two Brown women watched him walk from the restaurant.

Chapter Twenty-Three

"How is he?"

"Mama, he's as good as he can be. He misses you and he's sad, lonely and very disappointed in himself. He also realizes, finally, that you're done."

"I hope we aren't done. Aura I love your dad. He's been a part of my life for many years. I simply can't be his wife any longer. My prayer is that in time we can get along, enjoy you and baby Amy together. He's very important to me."

"Mama, you mean that don't you?"

"I absolutely mean it. What Brown, Black and I had for years was beautiful and respectful. No one seemed to understand it but us. Now I have no intentions of being with your dad intimately ever again, but I do want and need him in my life. Hopefully he'll find someone also."

"I sure do hope it isn't Andrea Wills."

"I'm sure it isn't. I think that was to try to make me jealous. She is lovely and as young as my daughter and if I had been any other woman I would probably have made a scene. He should know better."

"I don't think daddy should ever marry again. He's too..."

"How is Lady Amy?" Aura appreciated the change of subject.

"She's fine. She's enjoying the daycare, though she misses you."

"I know she does, but her nanny needs some down time and that little diva was wearing me out. I plan to pick her up tomorrow and keep her all night."

"Mama, I think I will take you up on your offer to move into the house. I can rent out my condo and it will give Amy some space to grow. When are you planning on moving?"

"I was actually planning to move before Christmas, but now with the date moved up on EP, I need to move sooner. I will probably simply get one of those waterfront places. I don't need much space."

"Besides, you won't need it for long."

"What does that mean?"

"Mama, come on, you know you and Malcolm Black are going to get married and you two aren't going to live in some condo by the ocean."

"That's true, he has several places. We will most likely make the cabin our main residence. It's beautifully remote and reflects both of us. Malcolm has several houses. Does my marrying him bother you?"

"No, ma'am, I think the two of you are more suited for each other. I just hate seeing dad in so much pain. Time heals all things. He's thinking about moving to Tampa."

"That doesn't surprise me at all. When he closed the Atlanta office, he had mentioned opening one in Tampa at that time. That would probably be good for him. I'm sure Jackie will be disappointed, having her favorite son leaving town."

"Have you spoken to grandma since you and dad split?"

"No, in fact she called me to ask me if she could come by the house later. She has never been a big fan of mine. According to her, Brown loved me too much, whatever that means. I did speak to Jefferson though. He's disappointed."

"I went by there the other day. I want Amy to know all of her folks. Grandma didn't say much, she did comment on how much like you I was. Granddaddy simply rolled his eyes and snuck Amy bits of candy."

"Have you spoken to Muha?"

"Yes, I asked him if he were coming for my 4th of July bash next week. He said he would, he also asked me to invite Ebony."

"Ebony, I thought he and Amber were trying to work things out?"

"They are but it seems Muhammad Brown is like his daddy. Amber is better for him but he and Ebony go back. Who knows? By the way Daddy is coming and Malcolm. I told daddy he could bring someone if he wanted to. Is that okay?"

"That's fine with me. Does Brown know you invited Malcolm?"

"He does, look mama I need to run, but I'll see you later."

"Okay baby…"

Chapter Twenty-Four

Cinnamon did a final inspection of the den. She had set up a table for her and Jackie to have refreshments. She knew Jackie would look around. She rarely came to visit, even for functions. Her preference was for her kids to come to her home. Cinnamon looked at all the accumulations of her life. Her home was filled with paintings, portraits and photos of her family and friends. Aura had taken several to her father. Prominently displayed were several photos that included Malcolm. Swallowing down a lump Cinnamon walked to answer the door. She knew Jackie would ring it several times. Jackie stood in the doorway, dressed in a dark blue pantsuit. She was a tall, spare woman with lovely brown skin and long grey and black tresses. She had looked pretty much the same all the years Cinnamon had known her. Cinnamon had always called her Jackie. She had told her that she only wanted to be called mama by her own children. That had suited Cinnamon just fine.

"Come in Jackie, I have prepared tea for us." Jackie walked in looking around. Cinnamon smiled at that. It pleased her that some things never changed. She watched her walk around picking up photos. Finally, she sat down at the table.

"This is very nice, looks like you were preparing for the queen."

"We're all queens, aren't we?" Jackie chose to ignore the remark. She poured herself some tea and took a couple of slices of cake.

"So, just like that you're going to throw away your marriage?"

"No ma'am, not just like that and *I'm* not throwing away anything. Brown and I have been successfully married for thirty-two years. I have never had to make a harder decision in my life. But Jackie this is the best decision for me."

"And it's all about you, isn't it?"

"I'm not sure I know what you mean?"

"Well, your mama and your aunts always thought the sun rose and the moon set in you. Brown was the same way, always indulging you, buying you everything. I tried to warn him. I guess you're trading up." Swallowing down fury, Cinnamon took a sip of water. She didn't want to disrespect her elder, but it was time to set the record straight.

"Listen to me Jackie, you're right, my mama and my aunts did think the world of me. Much the same as you do your children. And Brown didn't indulge me. Even the years I didn't work, I always contributed financially to my home. I have money, always have. I allowed you and others to think I was the pampered princess but that was never true. Let me get something straight, I don't need a man to take care of me financially, never have, never will. That's may be why you stayed married to Jefferson but it certainly isn't my motive for love or marriage."

"Well my son could have easily divorced you."

"He sure could have."

"It's not like you're Mrs. Innocent, you have been running around with that Malcolm Black for years."

"You're right again, Jackie, I'm not Mrs. Innocent. I am Cinnamon Dubois Brown and I'm not ashamed of anything I've ever done. What about you?"

"What does that mean?"

"It means that we have all sinned and fallen short of God's grace. Me, you, Brown and everyone else we know. I grew up in this town. There are no secrets under the sun. I know you." Draining her teacup, Jackie stood up.

"I knew I couldn't talk any sense into you. But remember, the grass isn't always greener on the other side."

"I'll keep that in mind. Let yourself out." Cinnamon sat at the table watching her mother-in-law depart. *I sure won't miss her…*

****

Several hours later the doorbell rang. Looking out the window, Cinnamon wasn't surprised to see Brown. She knew Jackie probably went by his office on the way home. Opening the door, she invited him in. He followed her to the kitchen,

106

watching her prepare tea. He walked over to her, taking her in his arms, kissing her passionately. Cinnamon gently pulled away. Her heart raced in her chest, he was still a very desirable man.

"You still want me…"

"We had a lot of problems but that wasn't one of them."

"Can I make love to you? You know how good we are together. Just one last time, I can't stop…"

"No…"

"So you cheated on me, but you won't cheat on him?"

"B, that isn't what this is about and you know it. I did make love to Black, while making love to you and I asked for forgiveness for that. For the past many months, while we were living together I didn't allow Malcolm to touch me. I don't want to do that again, it went against everything I believed in."

"Cinnamon, you're still my wife."

"Brown…" Backing away, he held up his hands in surrender.

"Okay, I'm certainly not going to force you, but it's nice to know you still want me."

"William Brown, what do you want, I know you didn't come all the way out here to prove I still find you desirable."

"No, I wanted to apologize for mama. She had no business coming out here. I can only imagine what she said."

"No need to apologize. Your mama is a grown woman. She simply stated what she has always felt. It was time for me to set her straight on a few things. It really frustrates me that they all think I just sit at home counting money while the men in my life work and pamper me. She thinks I married you for your money."

"I need to tell her it was for my big, fine body."

"Make sure you do that. Now go home."

"Okay, but it's your last chance to get some of this."

"Brown, take your big fine body out of here. You're too much." She heard him laughing on the way out the door. She had to smile. It was nice to tease with him.

Chapter Twenty-Five

Black had convinced Cinnamon to go for a drive. She didn't do well with surprises. He had even blindfolded her. After an hour's drive, he took her hand leading her from the car. Once he had her inside he pulled the blind from her face. Looking around she discovered she was inside a very lovely house. The walls were floor to ceiling bookshelves. The floors were polished marble and one wall of the living room faced the Atlantic Ocean. Her mouth flew open in joy.

"My goodness, what is this place?" He dangled keys in front of her face.

"This is your new home. Our new home once you marry me, but for now it is all yours." Running outside she ran through the tall sea grass to the water. He ran behind her. Wrapping his arms around her, he turned her around.

"This is so lovely. I don't know what to say."

"Say you will live here and that you aren't mad at me for doing this. It has been sitting empty for years. I would see it and think about buying it but the last thing I needed was another property. When you mentioned wanting to live at the ocean, I thought of this place. I brought Aunt Gladys and Aura out here and they both said you would love it." Tears poured from her eyes.

"Aura came out here with you. Are the two of you getting along?" He gently kissed the tears from her face.

"We are. I was worried about it, since she's such a daddy's girl but we're cool. We don't talk about her dad. Mostly we talk about business and basketball. She even invited me over for dinner one night with her and Amy."

"I'm glad. I knew she invited you over for the barbeque."

"Yes, I'm going to stop by. I won't stay long I don't want Brown uncomfortable."

"Black, I want you to stay as long as I stay. Everyone has got to get used to the fact that you and I are a couple."

"Are we going together?"

"Absolutely. She told me she didn't want me to do anything except show up and eat, so that's what I'm doing. Muhammad is going to be there also."

"Cool."

Chapter Twenty-Six

When Cinnamon and Black arrived at Aura's the party was in full swing. Muhammad was there. He walked over picking his mom up, swinging her around. He nodded at Black. Brown walked over, shaking Black's hand, intimately placing an open-mouth kiss on Cinnamon's lips. She glanced at Black, who winked at her, but there was a look in his eye. The yard was filled with mostly friends of Aura's. Cinnamon noticed Ebony was in attendance and she and Muhammad looked very much like a couple. She also noticed Muhammad was consuming a lot of beer. After several, she asked him if she could talk to him, privately. He followed her inside.

"So Muha, what's up with all the beer? I have never seen you drink so much."

"Mama, I'm a grown man, I don't need you getting in my business. So what if I have a few." Before she could answer Brown walked in.

"Boy, don't be disrespectful to your mama."

"She's disrespecting us. She brings her man here like it is cool." Tears almost choked Cinnamon.

"Muha, Malcolm has been a part of our lives for years."

"Muhammad, apologize to your mama."

"No Dad, you apologize to her. This is your damn fault. Maybe if you could have kept it in your pants she wouldn't be doing this. Both of you disgust me." He stormed out of the condo because he didn't want them to see him with tears in his eyes." Within minutes Aura and Black walked inside.

"What's going on, Muha just ran out of here with Ebony?" Aura asked. Brown shrugged his shoulders. Black looked at Cinnamon.

"He's hurt and angry. He doesn't want to accept that his dad and I are separate. He's going through a grieving process. He'll be okay. Was he driving?"

"No ma'am Ebony was."

"That's good. I'll leave if you want me to."

"No ma'am. We're all family, dysfunctional though we may be. Mama you're my mama, daddy you're my daddy and Malcolm you're going to be my stepfather. I have accepted that and Muhammad just needs to grow up. Mama I told you, you spoiled that boy. He needs to man up." The three of them chuckled slightly. The remainder of the day was anti-climactic. Several hours later, Muhammad returned, refusing to talk to anyone.

****

Driving home later Black asked Cinnamon if she wanted him to speak to Muhammad.

112

"No, I plan to talk to him tomorrow. He'll be okay. He's hurt. He's so young and feels he needs to take sides. He'll be fine."

"Is that the first time Brown kissed you on the mouth since he left?"

"No, it was the second time, why?"

"I don't know. It just bothered me a little bit."

"Let me get something straight right now. Just because I cheated on him with you, I'm not going to cheat on you with him. Understand!"

"Yes, ma'am! But that's not what I meant."

"What did you mean?" Cinnamon was struggling to keep the peevishness out of her voice.

"I don't know. I just felt he was trying to make a point. That he could kiss you whenever and however he wanted to."

"Black, he was trying to make a point. He wants you to think just that. Brown and I are done. It doesn't bother me if he greets me with a kiss, so long as he don't try running his tongue down my throat, or licking my face." Looking over at her, he had to laugh.

"Woman, you are too much and he practically did tongue kiss you..."

"No you are. When Brown and I were married you had no problem kissing me, knowing he was kissing me. I spent over a year going from kiss to kiss and from..."

"Cinnamon!"

"Well, it's true. I could hardly keep my mind straight. I was so damn glad when you decided to be celibate. I was about to invite you to move in the bed with me and Brown, it would have made it easier!" Looking at the indignant look on her face, he had to laugh. After several minutes she laughed with him.

"I'm sorry, but I don't want you and Brown kissing like that. There are too many memories..."

"Negro, I already told you..."

"Okay...but Brown got to kiss you for almost thirty years, just him. I want the same amount of time..."he looked at her, winking. She crossed her eyes, poking her tongue at him.

Chapter Twenty-Seven

The next morning Cinnamon went to Aura's to talk to Muhammad. Last night he had hurt her feelings, now it was time to straighten him out. She had warned Aura and she and the baby had vacated the premises. Walking into the guestroom she was a bit shocked to see Ebony in the bed with Muhammad. *He wants to do grown man things but acts like a child when thing don't suit him. I know Aura set him up. She wanted me to see this.* Cinnamon yanked the covers from the bed, startling them both awake. Ebony looked at Cinnamon, grabbing a sheet to cover up. It took Muhammad several minutes to fully wake up. By that time Cinnamon had opened the blinds, flooding the room with light. Ebony had grabbed her clothing, scampering downstairs. Cinnamon quietly said to her;

"I hope you're being safe." Unable to meet the older woman's eyes, she nodded as she fled from the room. Muhammad, now fully awake sat up in the bed with a smirk on his face, trying to hide his embarrassment.

"Mama, it's not what you think..."

"Muha, of course it is. You're almost twenty-four and sexually active. And it seems like you are active with at least two women, your fiancé and your former fiancé. I guess that would make you as disgusting as your father and I."

"Mama, I didn't mean that..."

"Of course you did. And it's your choice to be disgusted. Your father has had a slew of women as you know. Your mother for over a year had an affair with your father's friend, with Brown's permission, basically, but an affair non-the-less. However, for over a year now I have only been with your father. He decided to otherwise engage and I have decided to divorce him. Not just because I want to marry Malcolm and I do, but because I'm tired of being married to a serial cheater. If I'd had better sense I would have left Brown years ago. I didn't but now I have and you my son will have to deal with it, man up as your sister said. And my expectation is that you will treat Malcolm respectfully. He loves you and nothing about that has changed. Do you understand me?"

"Yes ma'am but can't I be hurt about everything I believed in changing?" He looked and sounded like a lost child.

"Of course you can but what you have to understand is that it changes nothing for you. I love you, your daddy loves you and Malcolm loves you. We are all going to be there as we always have."

Rubbing his eyes, he prepared to get up, realizing he was naked. He glanced at his mother. She stood quietly, arms folded, staring at him, finally grinning, "I can assure there's nothing under that sheet I haven't seen already, but go take a shower, then I want you to take me to breakfast. I want to get in your business." Grinning sheepishly he nodded at his mama, glad she wasn't mad at him.

"So Muha, tell me what's going on in your life?" Cinnamon and her son were sitting outside the Waffle and Chicken Palace. Looking directly at his mom, he swallowed down his food.

"Mama, don't ever stop calling me Muha. I remember when I was little you called me Muha-Luha. When you call me Muhammad I feel bad."

"When I call you Muhammad I want you to know I mean business, now answer my question."

"Well, I love Amber and want to get married but she's so complicated, ambitious and is so much work." 'Like me I guess,' Cinnamon thought.

"What does that mean?"

"She just completed her master's in economics and she's going to teach at UCLA. She already owns a house and has everything all planned out. I'm not ready to live like that."

"Then why ask her to marry you? Why not just play the field?"

"I didn't want to lose her. Mama I love her and she's wife material but I want to have some fun. You taught me how to handle my money and all that stuff. But I'm not even twenty-four yet."

"I suspect your daddy married me for the same reasons, he loved me and didn't want to lose me. He also thought I was too ambitious and his first thing to do was try to slow my ambitions and for a while it worked. But, in time we always become who we always were. If you don't plan to do right by her, hurt her now and let her go. And what is Ebony?" His eyes twinkled at the thought of her.

"Ebony is fun. She knows how to relax and just be. She wants to look good and feel good. She knows there is time for all that other stuff."

"But you don't want to marry her?"

"No, I don't. Ebony isn't marriage material, Amber is. I just don't know. Thankfully we didn't plan a big wedding. She's giving me until the end of the year to make up my mind."

"Hmm, Muha, does the fact that Amber earns twice as much as you have any bearing on this?" A look of discomfort passed quickly over his face.

"In a few years I'll be out-earning her…"

"Again, you're avoiding my question. Is that a part of the issue? Are you bothered by the fact that her salary will pay for most of what you have together, if so that is very old-school for someone supposedly so hip."

"Maybe, right now we both earn about the same, but once she starts teaching her salary will be over 100Gs. I guess it does bother me a bit."

"Well you have money that you could tap into when you turn twenty-five. Does she know about the money mama and Aunt Sara left you?"

"She knows about the money auntie left, but not what grandma left. I try not to even think about that."

"Why, it's a lot of money and it will certainly purchase a house or seven?" He grinned at his mother's words. The almost half a million his grandma left over six years ago was sitting in the bank collecting interest. He never even checked it. Being a smart woman, his grandma hadn't allowed them to inherit it until they were twenty-five. Aura still hadn't touched hers and she was almost thirty.

"Then my guess Muha-Luha is you aren't ready to be married. You just want to have fun. Take your time."

"I don't want to end up like Black."

"What does that mean?"

"Chasing down the woman I love for years because I was too stupid to marry her when I had the chance to."

"He has the chance to now."

"I know. Do you think I can stay with you tonight? I guess it will be the last time I sleep in my old room. That mean sister of mine told me she's going to turn it into an office."

"Absolutely."

Chapter Twenty-Eight

Cinnamon couldn't believe how far along the EP had come in the just six weeks. She had been working on it non-stop. She had also moved into the cabin by the ocean. She and Black were in a wonderful place. He wanted to move in with her but she wasn't going to allow that until they were married. She understood his fears but she was going to stick to her guns. She was done making decisions based solely on what someone else wanted. She was looking forward to opening EP in less than two weeks. The day after Labor Day was three months earlier than she had planned. Walking through she was very pleased with how everything was set up. There was a large meeting room in shades of blue, a moderate sized kitchen, an office/counseling room for her and a library. There was also a modern, yet old-fashioned jukebox. Her heart surged with joy at that. She had done it mostly on her own. Black's only contribution had been the jukebox and the resting/bathroom that he had talked the designers into adding to her office. She had been pleasantly surprised when she returned from a visit to Muha in California. She hadn't seen or heard from Brown in almost three weeks. According to Aura he was doing okay, he had dinner with her and Amy weekly. Turning in preparation to leave she saw Brown walking up the sidewalk. It was as if though she had thought him up. He looked as handsome as ever, though his stride was less confident. Cinnamon's heart turned over at the sight of him. It bothered her that he was struggling, particularly since she was so happy with her new life. There were moments when she struggled but mostly she was at peace. His face lit up at the sight of her.

"Hello C, how are you? Aura told me the place was done. I hope you don't mind me coming by to see it?" She embraced him lightly, inviting him in, taking him on a full tour. After they were done, she walked him back to the kitchen for a glass of tea.

"So B, how are you?"

"I'm okay. I miss you and my family but work is good and I'm making it. The doctor told me to watch my cholesterol and a few other things, but I'm good. I better because if I get sick, I'm on my own." He tried to joke but the pain was evident in his voice.

"No you wouldn't. B, you have to know that if anything happened to you I would be there for you. I don't have any ill will towards you. You're my first love, the father of my children, I'll always love you." His heart warmed at her words.

"But you'll never kiss me, make love to me or wrap your body around mine on cold winter nights, will you?"

"No B, I won't, but I'll always have those memories as will you." A slight grin appeared on his face.

"Memories, that's something I guess. I don't know if Aura told you, but I'm moving to Tampa in a month. I have found an office and that will be good for me. Center City is less than two hours to visit. Aura promised me that she and the baby will come down a lot and I told Mama I will eat with her and dad a couple times a month."

"Good for you. You never wanted to be here anyway. Tampa will be good for you, professional sports and night life. B?"

"Yeah, baby?"

"Do you think you will marry again?"

"I doubt it. I'm already married and always will be."

"You're a young, attractive man with a lot to offer an *understanding* woman." Glancing at her, he could see she was teasing him."

"I guess she would have to be *understanding*. Look, I'm going to head out but I will be here for your grand opening. Muhammad said he's coming and bringing Amber."

"Yes, he told me when I was out there. I hope they don't get married, he's not ready."

"He's too much like his old man." They allowed those words to linger between them. Kissing her gently on the cheek, he made his departure. *I love and miss her so much… it really is true that you don't miss your water until your well runs dry and God knows I miss her.*

Chapter Twenty-Nine

The night of the opening of Empowerment Place was beautiful. Half of Center City filtered through, congratulating Cinnamon on the opening. Though girls were doing well collectively, most venues were geared towards boys. Cinnamon's intent was to change that. She was very pleased to see Muhammad and Amber together. Aura, Amy and Aunt Gladys were all beaming with pride. Black's family was all in attendance. He was so filled with being a part of this. When he and Cinnamon had started planning this a couple years earlier, he'd had no idea she would be months away from marrying him. He stood near the window watching her stoppmingle. She looked particularly lovely in an almond colored dress. She had removed her wedding band and finally had his ring on her ring finger. Joy filled his heart at the sight of her.

"She's absolutely beautiful, isn't she?" The sound of Brown's voice startled him. Turning, he looked at him, he was further surprised to see Khadijah Owa with him. She had been Brown's mistress and employee for years. It had ended badly when she had tried to blackmail Brown. Black hadn't seen her in years. She had also formerly worked for Black Enterprises. She was a tall, stately African woman in her late fifties. She nodded at Black.

"Yes, she's the loveliest. How are you doing man?" Khadijah discreetly walked away so the men could talk.

"I'm healing. Officially divorced, but hanging in there." Surprise sprung in Black's mind, Cinnamon hadn't told him the divorce was final.

"So what are you planning and how is Tampa?"

"Tampa is good, low key. I'm going to work a couple more years, then, I don't know, my plans have changed…" Nodding, Black looked towards Khadijah.

"I like her man, I always have. When I got to Tampa I found out her husband had passed away. I called her and she moved to Tampa. Her son lives there. Man, she's low maintenance. She's not Cinnamon, but who is?"

"Hello Khadijah." Khadijah turned to the sound of Cinnamon's voice.

"Hello Cinnamon, you're as beautiful as ever."

"As are you, please look around and get some food. Thanks for coming." Khadijah was startled at the genuine warmth in Cinnamon's voice. She smiled slightly, preparing to walk away.

"Khadijah…"

"Yes?"

"Be good to him." Nodding she walked away.

"Hello, Mrs. Brown." Cinnamon grinned at her, now ex-husband.

"Hey B." Leaning towards him, she pulled him into an embrace. "Thanks for signing the papers."

"It was the hardest thing, I have ever done. But I know it was all left to do. Thirty two years down the drain." Cinnamon swallowed a lump, blinking back tears.

"Not down the drain B. We had some wonderful years, two amazing kids and Lady Amy. What we had is forever."

"Thanks for saying that, it means a lot to me. I will always love you."

"And I you. I'm glad to see you with someone."

"Even her?"

"Especially her, she's lovely and *understanding.*" The two of them looked at each other and howled with laughter. Everyone in the room looked towards them. Many were surprised. The family members were pleased, especially Black.

Chapter Thirty

Black and Cinnamon arrived at the ocean about midnight. He had to shake her awake when they arrived. Once inside, he asked her if he could stay.

"Of course, I have a surprise for you. Let me take a shower and I'll be with you in a few." He walked around looking at how lovely Cinnamon had made the place. A few of the furnishings were from her home, a few others were family heirlooms, but most were things the two of them had purchased together. Everything in the bedroom and kitchen was new. It had really touched him that Cinnamon had chosen to do that.

"Hey handsome..." He looked up to see Cinnamon changed into a white lace nightgown. "Get down on one knee..." Looking at her, he decided to play along. Once on his knee she handed him an envelope. Looking inside, he saw the divorce decree, ending the marriage of William Jefferson Brown and Cinnamon Lee Dubois Brown. Tears poured down his face at what this meant. Looking up he could see that her face was wet as well.

"Cinnamon Lee Dubois, will you marry me?"

"Malcolm Black, Cinnamon Lee Dubois would be honored to become Cinnamon Dubois Black."

"Word..."

"Word...."

"Now before we make this legal, can we sin a little bit?" Her eyes lit up with pleasure and desire. Standing he picked her up.

"I though you would never ask."

Chapter Thirty-One

"Mama and daddy are divorced." Aura's words penetrated Muhammad's brain. The two of them were sitting outside on the back porch. Something they had done so many times over the years. Neither had ever thought it would be Aura's home.

"Wow. That's hard to believe. They seem to be getting along okay. I was surprised he bought Ms. Owa.

"Not me. Daddy needs someone. Not only that I think he needed mama to see him with someone. He's far from happy, but he's trying."

"Well, mama looked beautiful and really happy. In fact I have never seen her happier. It seems like she's free."

"Muha, she is free. Mama has always done the right thing. She fell in love with daddy and married him. She had us and took care of us then she moved here and started taking care of grandma and the elders. For years she moved at daddy's whims. Even though she loved teaching, it really wasn't her thing. Mama is a free-spirited writer, entrepreneur type. Writing and the Center is who she is. She's happy and free."

"What about Malcolm Black."

"He's perfect for her. Muha, he adores her and won't get in the way of or be threatened by her. He will take care of her. He has nothing to prove to anyone, all he wants is her. I watched him last night. His eyes followed her every move but he left her alone and he was so proud. Not only that but he looked genuinely happy to see mama and daddy getting along. He's a good man."

"He is. I remember all those years I saw him around mama when grandma was sick. You could see how much he loved her. She didn't seem to notice it. But there were times when they would sit side by side and...I think daddy's a fool. I'm really mad at him, I don't want to be, but I am."

"I understand that, but daddy is daddy. So what is up with you and your women?"

"Amber and I are trying, as you can see, she's not sleeping with me. Ebony is pissed because Amber is with me. It is what it is. " Standing, he hugged his sister before walking inside.

Chapter Thirty-Two

Brown stood at his office window looking out at the lake surrounding his office. He had everything, financial success, wonderful kids and extended family, everything except Cinnamon. Most days he was fine but there were times when he didn't think he could live through the pain. Khadijah provided some solace but she wasn't his wife, his ex-wife. Picking up the Tampa Tribune and seeing the engagement announcement had almost knocked him off his feet:

Millionaire Malcolm Douglass Black announced his engagement to bestselling author, Cinnamon Lee Dubois Brown. They are planning a spring wedding. The usually reclusive Black spoke openly to reporters about the upcoming nuptials, "I'm finally marrying the woman of my heart, my dreams." He wouldn't disclose any details but rumor has it they are planning an island wedding.

"William..." Cinnamon's voice penetrated his consciousness. Turning, he was startled to see her standing in his office. She was casually dressed in a denim dress. He hadn't seen her in the almost two months since EP had opened. Her hair was growing out and curling around her face. The fact that she looked so lovely and happy shot an arrow through his heart.

"Hey baby, what brings you by?" He restrained himself from taking her in his arms. That would have been his undoing.

"I'm actually here with Aura. She came down to sign some contracts with one of her Tampa Bay clients. Ms. Amy is visiting with Ryoko this week. Aura really wants her to know her biological mother. EP is closed this week and next week for Thanksgiving so she asked me to ride down here with her. She told me your office was right here, so I decided to invite you to lunch." He smiled at her efforts.

"Where is Malcolm?" Giggles spewed forth from her. She knew he would ask that.

"He's at home. The Learning Center is open this week. What are you doing next week for Thanksgiving?"

"I plan to spend the day with mom and dad. Friday it'll be back to work."

"Well, if you want you are welcome to stop by Aunt Gladys'. We're all gathering there for a late dinner. You're still very much a part of this family. Amy and Muha won't be there, but Aura, Malcolm and I will."

"I just might do that. Black won't mind will he?"

"Did you mind when he ate with us last year?" He laughed at her audacity.

"Touche'"

"So, do you want lunch or no?"

131

"I do." Walking out Cinnamon smiled at Khadijah, who threw a questioning glance towards Brown. He chose to say nothing.

After getting settled at the restaurant and ordering, Brown asked Cinnamon about EP. Her face lit from the inside out.

"It's so wonderful. I love having the girls there. Some are so challenging, but it's awesome. I have never done better work in my life."

"You look good. I'm happy for you and I miss you so much. Do you ever miss me?"

"Of course I do. But B, I love my life."

"And him."

"And him. He misses you also."

"I miss him as well. Ironically, I was never closer to another brother. But I'm not ready to spend the night with the two of you."

"We aren't ready for that either. But we aren't living together."

"So does that mean I can spend the night with you?"

"No, it does not. You're a mess. What's up with you and Ms.Owa? Malcolm told me her husband passed away."

"He did, we're fine. I enjoy her. She doesn't require much."

"Unlike your ex-wife, the high maintenance Cinnamon, who was a lot of work?" He heard the fun in her voice.

"My wife…look, I have a meeting in a few minutes, thanks for this. I might stop by over the holidays."

"That would be nice. I plan to wait here for Aura."

Aura breezed in, sitting down beside her mom. Cinnamon had ordered lunch for her.

"So, how did it go?"

"Like taking candy from a baby, I went by dad's office. He and Ms. Owa were in a heated discussion."

"Probably, because he took off with his ex-wife."

"So, how was that?"

"It was fine, Brown isn't as happy as I would like for him to be and it's particularly hard for me because I'm as happy as I can be. He had the wedding announcement on his desk when I walked in, that had to be hard for him. Malcolm has splashed them all over the Florida newspapers."

"I was surprised at that, he's usually so closemouthed. I had never seen a photo of him in a newspaper of magazine. I know that the mags have been after him for years."

"He has always said that if I married him, he would splash it everywhere and he has."

"How does it feel to be loved like that?" Cinnamon eyes held her daughter's.

"It feels awesome, nothing compares to it. Your daddy really loved me Aura but there were so many conditions. I never realized how tightly I held myself until I moved back to Center City, in some ways it was as though I was scared of him. He often told me what to do and how to do it and because I loved him I complied. But when I changed, there was no turning back. The beauty of Malcolm is he loves me just as I am… the good, the bad and the ugly, the light and the dark."

"I want that…"

"I want that for you. Do you ever talk to Ryoko?" Pain flickered across Aura's brow.

"Occasionally, I have spoken to her more in the past few days than in years because she has Amy. Last night Amy told me she wanted to come home. There is no bond between her and Ryoko and no family around."

"So her parents still haven't come around?"

"No, I don't suspect they will. They have no use for the baby of their lesbian daughter, from her former lover's brother's sperm. Especially since the child is Black." Cinnamon could feel Aura's pain."

"Do you still love her?"

"No, I don't, not like that. She hurt me too bad, running out when things were tough. It has really messed me up. I have been on a few dates but nothing serious, but sometimes I'm really lonely. Mom I wish I were straight, seems like it would be easier." Cinnamon knew that wasn't true, love was hard, period.

"We will simply have to pray about it. I love you sweetie." Draining her glass, Aura stood up.

"Are you ready to go?" I'm sure your Black Knight is ready for me to bring you home."

"I'm sure he is. We are fussing a bit. He wants to run off and get married but I'm going to wait until June."

"Why?"

"Because I want to, I made reservations for Jamaica. There will only be you, Amy, Muha, Aunt Gladys and Alexandra on my side. Black is bringing his sisters, brothers and his nephews. He has to be patient."

"Where is Aunt Xan? I have barely seen her in months."

135

"She's living down the coast with Lynn, mostly. Once she retired she was more mobile. I rarely see her myself, but I'm glad she has a life. Come on sweetie, let's go."

Chapter Thirty-Three

"So we can't move the date up and we can't live together?" Cinnamon removed her legs from Malcolm's lap. She was getting a bit put out with the same questions over and over again.

"That's right. Malcolm we're getting married in June and you practically live her now. You stay here three or four nights a week. You have as many clothes here as I do. Why can't you be patient?"

"Patient, woman I have been as patient as Job. I just don't see what the big deal is unless you don't plan to marry me."

"You know better than that..." Malcolm Black stood up walking from the porch. He walked inside and started taking his clothes from the closet.

"Black Man, what are you doing?"

"I'm moving my stuff, I don't want to crowd your space and I won't spend any more nights over here. How is that?" Cinnamon was completely stunned at his tone.

"Come on tell me what's wrong with you..." She wrapped her arms around him, not allowing him to move until he relaxed.

"I'm scared. I have never been so frightened in my life. When I'm not with you, I'm afraid something will happen...I hate feeling this way. Cinnamon I have never been this close to having what I want..."

"Don't be scared. I just want to do this how I'm doing it and I don't want to be manipulated. Malcolm, I love you, I love when you stay here with me and I love having your clothes hang in my closet, but I need you to wait so we can do this the way I planned. Please."

"Okay..."

"Now put your clothes back in the closet and stop acting like that." She started tickling him until he started laughing. Once he was loose she started kissing him on his face and teasing him.

"You're such a baby, throwing a tantrum, you surprised me, I just told Aura a couple of days ago how you love me so unconditionally."

"I do love you unconditionally, but I want to marry you. I want you to be Mrs. Black, I have taken too many chances with your love and when I'm not with you, I'm so damn worried that something will take you away from me, again."

"The only thing that can come between us is leaving the planet and if you keep acting up, you will be leaving the planet."

"Promise?"

"Promise, now why don't we say our vows right now between the two of us, and then when we're done, can you kiss me from head to toe?"

"I can do that..."

Chapter Thirty-Three

Who in the world can be knocking at my door?
Cinnamon thought as she prepared to leave home.
Peering through the window she saw a tall woman
in her early sixties and a man of about thirty-five
standing on her doorstep. Opening the door, she
didn't recognize either, but the man looked familiar.
He was quite tall, handsome with velvety dark-
chocolate skin.

"Hello Mrs. Brown, I am Amelia Broaai and this
is my son Malcolm." Cinnamon's heart raced in her
chest. Glancing at the young man again, she knew
who he reminded her of. He looked like a young
Malcolm Black. *Oh my God, Malcolm has a son!
Who is this woman and why now?*

"Mrs. Broaii, do I know you?" The older woman
looked at Cinnamon, her eyes never wavering.

"Can we come in?" Moving back from the
doorway, Cinnamon waved them inside. Something
told her they wouldn't be harmful to her. She
watched them glancing around.

"Please have a seat. I was on my way out.
Please allow me to call my assistant to tell her I'm
running late. Can I get you something?"

Cinnamon's usual cool was completely
shattered. Malcolm had always bemoaned the fact
that he never had children, but yards away was a
full grown man, who was the spitting image of him.
After making her calls and preparing glasses of tea,
she walked back into the family room where her

139

uninvited guests waited. She served them then sat down across from them.

"Now... how can I help you?" The young man finally decided to speak up.

"Mrs. Brown we are sorry about this but until last month I knew myself to be Malcolm Broaai, however, when my father passed away my mother decided it was time to tell me that my real father was Malcolm Black. Mr. Black and my mother, it seems had an affair when he was a student at FAMU and she was a faculty member. Because she was married she never told him she was pregnant with his child. She chose to stay married to my father. The reason we are here at your home, is because I saw the announcement of your upcoming nuptials, we were unable to find any kind of listing for him." Cinnamon sat looking at the couple speechless. She didn't know what to say. Glancing at the mother, she could see how difficult this was for her.

"What exactly is it you wish for me to do?" This time Mrs. Broaii, spoke.

"We simply want you to ask Malcolm if he will speak with his son. I'm sure he has nothing to say to me, but Malcolm II was an innocent in this." Malcolm II chose to interject.

"Please, Mrs. Brown this is very important to me. I always felt like a stranger in my own home. My father was a stern Haitian man who didn't communicate with me very often. He was very close to my older sisters, but never to me and I often wondered why. I was also much taller and darker than he. I just assumed it was because my mother was also taller and darker. Now I understand." Glancing at Mrs. Broaii, Cinnamon, asked,

"So did your husband know Malcolm II, wasn't his son?"

"He knew... his only condition was that I never tell our son." Cinnamon's heart turned at the pain in her voice.

"I really need to leave now. Where are you staying?" The mother and son stood in unison.

"We are at the Center City Inn."

"I will have Malcolm contact you." They both thanked her as they walked out. Cinnamon was completely unsure how Malcolm would deal with this. He had spent his whole life feeling he would never have a child, when for over thirty years he'd had a son.

Chapter Thirty-Four

Cinnamon had been churning all day with how to break the news to Malcolm. When speaking to him earlier in the day he had caught something in her voice. She had explained it away as being busy. Now that she was on her way to the cabin, she was so nervous, she felt nauseous. Malcolm was known for losing his cool when he felt manipulated, and this was huge. She was still unsure how she felt about the news. Pulling into the driveway, she took her time getting out of the vehicle. Malcolm appeared on the porch. He was still dressed for business, sans the jacket and tie. Her heart turned over at how much like him the young man she had met only a few hours ago looked. Arriving on the porch, he pulled her into his arms kissing her fervently, her knees buckled with desire.

"Come on inside..." Pulling his lips from hers he looked into her eyes.

"What's wrong baby?" Tears appeared in her eyes as she walked inside with him on her heels. He sat down pulling her onto his lap.

"Talk..."

"Do you know Amelia Broaii?" Turning her around to face him, she saw a wary look in his eye.

"I used to. She was my Haitian studies professor in my senior year at FAMU. Why?"

"Were you in love with her?"

"No Cinnamon, I wasn't in love with her. She was a very lovely, very married, instructor, who I had an ill advised fling with. I broke it off with her after a few times because she claimed to be falling in love and I wasn't. She was twenty-nine and according to her unhappily married. I was twenty and not a very good man at the time. Sex was sex for sex's sake. Now tell me why."

"Well...it seems that she had a child...your child..." Malcolm abruptly stood up, nearly spilling Cinnamon on the floor.

"What did you say!?" A vein was pulsating in his forehead.

"I said it seems that she had a child with you. This morning she showed up on my doorstep with a man of about thirty-five and he is the spitting image of you." She watched him doing the calculations in his head. She saw resignation, acceptance and sadness cross his brow." Pulling her back down on his lap, she felt his heart beating rapidly.

"He actually looks like me?"

"He looks just like you, and his name is Malcolm."

"Lord, why did they come to you?"

"They saw the wedding announcements and couldn't find you. It seems he didn't know until a month ago when the man he thought was his father died." She felt Malcolm sobbing, she wrapped her arms around him to provide comfort.

143

"How could she do this to me? Other than to marry you, the only thing in the world I ever wanted was my own children, a son. For all those years she kept him from me. How could she?"

"Black Man, I'm sure she had many reasons. He wants to talk to you. They are at the Center City Inn."

"How will this affect us?" She could hear fear in his voice. Looking straight into his eyes and hopefully his heart she answered.

"This won't affect us. If he's your son, he'll be a part of our families. Whatever you want or need me to do, let me know and I will do that." He leaned into her kissing her passionately.

"Do you think this is about money?"

"Malcolm, I don't know. He didn't look poor. He looked and sounded educated but he was very sad because he has been betrayed as long as you have. His mother seemed fearful. So why did I never hear about her?"

"There was nothing to tell. She was faculty and I was a student. She was lonely and fine and I was the G-Spot player. When I ended it, I didn't see her at all."

"I thought you always practiced safe sex?" He chuckled sadly.

"I did, however, there was one time when there was an accident. I got myself tested for STDs and

144

moved on. That was prior to AIDS so I wasn't really worried. Also, the fact that she was married made me think she was being safe. How stupid!"

"Not stupid, just young and horny."

"So, you aren't going to leave me, now that you know I might be a baby-daddy?"

"Umm, umm, unless someone is pregnant now..."

"Not hardly, but come on over to that bed and I will try to make you pregnant." Giggling she stood up racing to the bed.

"Now that would be a miracle..."

"I believe in miracles..."

"Ummm..."

Chapter Thirty-Five

"I want you to go with me." Malcolm sat down on the bed next to Cinnamon. He had been up for hours, thinking about having a son, a grown man.

"Are you sure?" Cinnamon asked, sleepily.

"Positive, I want to strangle that woman and I need you there as a calming presence. We are meeting them at Aura's office at ten."

"At Aura's, why?"

"She's my attorney and I will need paternity tests and if he's my son, I will need to calculate how much I owe in child support and college tuition." Cinnamon fell out laughing. Malcolm looked at her not joining her in laughter. She hit him with the pillow and fell out laughing again.

"Cinnamon, what's so funny?"

"Negro you are. You're the most practical and honorable man. You have already calculated out child support and college tuition for a child you didn't even know you had. That's funny when brothers are running away from children they know are theirs. You're as funny as heck. I had better go with you. Otherwise you will have them signing a contract." She rubbed her belly. "And in case you knocked me up last night I need to save some money for our baby." She started giggling again, this time he threw the pillow at her and laughed with her.

Malcolm and Cinnamon was a picture of love and togetherness walking into Aura's office. He was dressed in a shark grey suit and she had on a dove gray ensemble. When they entered Aura was sitting behind her desk. To the left side of her was Amelia Broaii. Malcolm nodded at her. She looked at him, saying, "Hello Malcolm, I'm so sorry."

"Save it!" Cinnamon placed her hand in his as they sat down. Within moments Malcolm Broaii walked in the room and time stood still. He was dressed in dark grey slacks and a white button down shirt. There was no question that Malcolm Black was his father. Malcolm stood to his feet, looking at the younger man who was the spitting image of him. The young man stared back with tears pouring down his face. He offered Malcolm his hand, Malcolm walked to him pulling into an embrace. Both men stood, holding the other with sobs racking their bodies. The three women also had tears running down their faces. Mrs. Broaii stood, running from the room. Cinnamon ran out behind her. They were both out of breath when Cinnamon caught her. Cinnamon pulled her into an embrace, holding her tightly. After several minutes they sat down on a bench across from the pond.

"He hates me doesn't he?"

"No, he doesn't but he's hurt. There's nothing he wanted more than a child and to now discover he has one, has thrown him from a loop." Nodding she peered at Cinnamon curiously.

"You are that young girl he was so in love with aren't you?"

"All grown up…"

"So the two of you are now getting married?"

"Yes we are. Amelia, is it okay if I call you Amelia?"

"Yes."

"Please call me Cinnamon. Amelia, what does your son want from Malcolm?"

"He wants to know where he belongs. Chastain wasn't cruel to him, but he didn't love him either. Malcolm grew up quietly, immersed in books and music. He has two degrees in music and in computer science. He has a small, successful business in Panama City. He doesn't need Malcolm's money. He earns well and he has a small inheritance from Chastain. He just wants to know his father. Do you think Malcolm will ever forgive me?"

"I'm sure he will, but does it really matter, if this is about Malcolm II?"

"That's a fair question. It does because this isn't the first time I mislead him. He didn't know I was married when I first went after him."

"Oh…Did you get pregnant on purpose? Were you in love with him?"

"Yes I was in love with him and no I didn't get pregnant on purpose. However, as soon as I realized how pregnant I was I knew he was the father. I am Catholic, so abortion wasn't a consideration. My husband never forgave me and I paid penance for years."

"My heart goes out to you but it's not comparable to what the Malcolms have had to endure." Amelia heard clearly what Cinnamon was saying, though she said it softly and kindly.

"I know, please tell my son I will see him at the hotel."

Malcolm stared at his son, unable to speak. The younger man babbled trying to explain his reasons.

"Sir, I don't want or need anything from you. I have my own. I simply need to know my father. Ms. Brown has drawn my blood for the tests. Please try to understand and try not to judge my mother too harshly. No one is more confused by this than I am but I'm trying." Nodding, Malcolm cleared his throat.

"I'm not there yet. If you're my son and I think you are. Your mother made a decision to keep that from me, from us. I'm sorry if I don't understand that. I could have died without ever knowing you. She knew me well enough to know how important family and kids were to me. I often talked to her of having a family when I was married."

"Did you consider marrying her?"

149

"No...I don't mean that disrespectfully but I wasn't in love with your mother. At first I didn't even know she was married. When I found out, I ended it."

"Thanks sir. I need to check on my mother, but when the results are back..." Malcolm stood up embracing the younger man again.

"When this is resolved, I want you to meet your family. Where will you be?"

"I'm taking my mother back to Tallahassee today but I work for myself, so my schedule is loose."

"What do you do?"

"I own a computer and music design company. Right now there is just me and two others but we are growing." Black was stunned at the pride that entered his heart. Hugging the young man again, he watched him depart. He slumped back into his chair. Within minutes Aura walked in.

"Step-D, are you okay." Smiling at her he loved the new nickname she had for him.

"Yeah, I think I will be. I need you to run a thorough background check on him." Smiling in commiseration she pulled a folder from behind her back, handing it to him.

"Thanks sweetie. This is between us?"

"Of course…"

"What are you two conspiring about?"
Cinnamon walked back in the room. The two of
them turned to her guiltily. They both knew she
wouldn't approve of the background check.

"Cinnamon Bun, you know this is lawyer, client
information. Don't be so snoopy." For some reason
those words rubbed Cinnamon the wrong way.
Turning on her heel she walked fast from the room.
Glancing at Aura, who shrugged her shoulders,
Malcolm took off after her.

Chapter Thirty-Six

Malcolm was literally trotting, trying to catch Cinnamon, even in a form-fitting dress and two inch heels she was power walking towards the Learning Center at a very fast pace. His heart was racing in his chest, trying to figure out what had set her off. She had looked infuriated at Aura's words.

"Cinnamon!"

She never looked back, continuing to almost sprint.

"Damn it Cinnamon, stop it!" It didn't bother him one bit that people in passing cars and pedestrians were looking at him as though he were demented. He felt demented. In just twenty-four hours his life had been turned upside down and somehow in all this he had infuriated Cinnamon. He watched her walk into the Learning Center. Knowing where she was going, allowed him to slow down a bit. When he reached the door he was stunned that she had locked it. He knocked on the door for several minutes. Searching through his pockets he realized his keys were a mile away at Aura's office. Turning around he was pleased to see Aura drive up in his car.

"Thank you. What in the world did I say wrong?" Aura giggled at the perplexed look on his face.

"I'm sure she will tell you. Mama is something else. Most of the time she is as cool as chilled cucumber, but every now and then she goes beserk, at least that's what Muha called it. I just called it mama. Leave her alone and she'll tell you. If you say something to her while she's hot, she'll probably hit you." Black smiled, remembering a couple years ago when he had made an offhand remark. Cinnamon had slapped him so hard his dark face had colored. Shocks of desire ran through him at the memory. He was unable to meet Aura's eyes. She giggled knowingly.

"So you have already seen and felt a bit of her, ummm, passion, huh?" She fell out laughing at his inability to look at her.

"Okay, I'm going to stroll back to my office. I hope to see you soon. And by the way Malcolm is a good man, his background is sterling. His mother on the other hand is something else."

"Okay, do you want me to drive you?"

"Uh, uh, go handle your business." He laughed at her use of her mother's favorite phrase.

Walking inside the building he could smell Addict perfume mingled with Cinnamon's sweat. Checking the library he didn't see her, he ran upstairs to the office and she wasn't sitting there. When he got back downstairs, he walked into the kitchen. She was sitting with her feet on the table, eating from a pint of Ben and Jerry's Vanilla Bean, savoring every bite, staring off into space. He didn't say a word. He swallowed down the desire that was bubbling within. She looked so beautiful and sexy with her bare feet and pink toe nails, and that spoon going in and out of her mouth…he went over to the cabinet retrieving a second spoon. Glancing at him, she handed him the ice cream, taking his spoon, allowing him to eat with the one she was using. For several minutes they didn't say a word, simply swapping the carton back and forth between them. Once they were done Black ventured to ask her what had happened.

"It made me mad that you and Aura were trying to hide something from me. I know all about client privilege. But, I'm your wife... uh I mean I'm going to be your wife..." He smiled at her words. It was the first time she had called herself his wife.

"You are my wife..." Rolling her eyes at him, she continued;

"Anyway, I know you two. There was never any question in my mind that you would run a background check, as you should. You are worth millions. I just don't appreciate either of you assuming you *know* how I'm going to feel about something."

"Baby, I wasn't trying to do that. I know you and you're a softie when it comes to family and you're already more sold on that boy than I am." A ghost of a smile appeared on her face.

"I am but I'm also a business woman..."

"You are...now, what else is bothering you?"

"I'm jealous..." He was stunned at her words.

"Of Malcolm..."

154

"Of course not, of Amelia. You and your ethnic women, Khadijah, was African, Margaret, Jamaican and now your long lost love shows up and she's Haitian. I guess that makes me plain old red beans and rice American." He could hear a bit of laughter in her voice. He sidled over closer to her, whispering in her ear.

"Woman you know I love me some red beans and rice, especially when it's spicy, hot and full of juice. I love dipping my breadstick down in there and savoring every bite, then licking the bowl." Shivers ran through Cinnamon at his words but she wasn't going to let him off the hook so easily.

"You didn't address the long lost love part."

"That woman isn't my love, long lost or otherwise. We had sex several times, one time of which the condom broke. I haven't thought of her or any woman in years. You got me so sprung and crazy. It takes all I got to keep up with you. Don't you know how much I love you?"

"How much?"

"I would give it all up for you, even getting to know my son."

"Now that's too much power for one woman to have..."

"It is what it is..."

"I don't want you to give anyone up. I just want you to love me and only me when it comes to the man woman thing…"

"You got it…now when are you going to marry me?"

"March…" Pleased shock entered his heart.

"Word!"

"Umm hmm."

"I guess I should make you jealous more often." Reaching over she slapped him, not lightly.

"Don't even try it. What you need to do is feed me."

"What you want red beans and rice?"

"Umm umm, that's for you, I want that breadstick…"

Chapter Thirty-Six

Malcolm sat on the balcony of Cinnamon's cabin reading through the file. Cinnamon was inside sleeping. After formally making up and having a leisurely dinner, they had both fallen asleep. He had woken, remembering the file Aura had given to him. He was pleased at how thorough it was. It seemed that Malcolm Broaii had never been in a bit of trouble. His school records described him as brilliant and introverted. He had worked eight years for Microsoft, returning to Florida seven years ago to start his own business. Malcolm smiled at that. Though, he had been something of a ladies man, he had never been married, engaged or had any children. His company was earning a nice six figure profit.

Amelia Broaii on the other hand had retired early due to several accusations of assignations with her students. In one instance the school had been sued and lost the case. She had also been personally sued. The student had recovered almost three hundred thousand dollars from her. What was most interesting is that her husband had left her over two hundred thousand. Malcolm suspected that she'd had to turn over her entire inheritance to the lawyers. She was probably doing okay on her retirement, but he was sure that twenty one years of back child support from a millionaire would come in handy at this time in her life. He would have to talk to Cinnamon about it. To him it was just money and he didn't care one way or the other. If Malcolm II was his son, he simply wanted to be part of his life. He felt Cinnamon's presence before he saw her. He patted his lap for her to sit down.

"Are you okay, Black Man, I turned over to take advantage of you and you were gone."

"Sorry I missed that. I was reading through the file Aura gave me. Did you know she calls me Step-D?"

"Yea, my kids and I have a habit of naming people we value."

"It's a loving habit. Malcolm is as good as gold, Ms. Broaii has some issues." He filled Cinnamon in on what he had learned.

"Wow, that's something. I guess she wouldn't be interested in you nowadays, you're too old for her." They chuckled together.

"Good… it seems she might be interested in my money. There was really no reason to tell him at this point I was his father. It seems she has a history of lying and manipulating. I just pray he isn't in on it."

"Malcolm, my gut tells me he isn't. Just tread carefully until you know what's up. You have never gone wrong before."

"Of course I have. All that money I gave Margaret, even Schae. They both knew I feel I have too much and weighed in on that. Mrs. Broaii knows the same thing. She knows that she doesn't have a leg to stand on legally but her hope is probably that she can use my feelings and her son's to get what she wants. I hope I'm wrong, but I'm sure I'm not."

"It's always something isn't it? But to whom much is given, much is expected and we have so much."

"We do, don't we." He wrapped his arms around her, pushing the recliner on full recline. He held her in his arms until they both fell asleep. The full sun in the sky woke them the next morning.

Chapter Thirty-Seven

"Hello."

"Hey Step-D, it seems like you are a daddy." Malcolm's heart rate sped up at Aura's words. For the past two weeks he had been sitting on pins and needles waiting for the results. He hadn't told a soul. The only people who knew other than the Broaii's were Cinnamon and Aura. That's exactly how he had wanted it until he knew for sure. He knew it was time to plan something with his family. Christmas was two weeks away and he and Cinnamon were going away with baby Amy and Jock after Christmas. They were going to spend Christmas day at Aura's house. This was her first venture at cooking for a large group. Muhammad was coming with Amber. Brown surely would be in attendance. It had been weeks since anyone had seen him.

"Wow, I don't even know what to say. I guess I should go out and get some cigars or something." Aura laughed at how innocent he sounded.

"You better tell Cinnamon Bun, so she can plan something."

"You right. She's at EP today. I better call her."

"Hey Black Man…"

"Hey baby, it seems like the boy is mine."

"Woo Hoo! So when are we having the coming out party and who are we inviting?" He was pleased by her enthusiasm. He didn't know how to feel.

"This will be quite small. Darrell and his wife, Delia and her kids and Jock will be there. Now that he lives with his dad most of the time, I'm concerned about him. I have partial custody and he might feel as though Malcolm will replace him. He's fifteen and real sensitive right now, otherwise just you, me, Aura and Malcolm II."

"What about Amelia?"

"That will be up to Malcolm. My preference would be for her not to be there, but that's his mother."

"Let's invite her. It will give me and Aura an opportunity to pick her brain." He smiled at his woman, she was always thinking.

Chapter Thirty Eight

The night of the dinner party the weather was perfect, warm and sultry for the middle of December. Cinnamon had decided to entertain at the oceanfront cabin. Malcolm had balked at it, calling it their love den. Cinnamon had reminded him that everywhere was their love den, but mostly the cabin in the woods. This was the first place they officially owned together and she wanted to open it up to family. He was amazed at how much she had done in a week. The once empty living room was now filled with plants and soft jade leather furnishings. The dining area had an informal pine dining table, with mixed chairs to seat sixteen. The scent of lemongrass and mint candles wafted through the air. There was also the fragrance of gumbo and jambalaya. Cinnamon looked lovely in a mint green, long flowing dress and emerald colored sandals. Black was dressed casually, for him, in cream and brown linen. He was a nervous as a cat on a hot tin roof.

In attendance by six was Aura, Amy, his brother Darrell, Darrell's wife Shelia, his sister Delia, her grown children Mikal and Sasha and fifteen year old Jacques, known as Jock.

"Well I'm sure everyone is wondering what this is all about, especially so close to Christmas…" before Black could finish speaking, the doorbell chimed. Cinnamon walked over to answer it. She walked in with Amelia Broaii closely behind her. There was a collective gasp when Malcolm II walked in. Cinnamon's eyes caught Jock's, he was who she was most concerned about. He had lived

162

with Malcolm for a couple of years but the last year had found him living with his dad. His older sister was at college. They were the children of Black's sister who had died from leukemia. He struggled with living with his father most of the time. He still saw Malcolm daily and he participated in all of his activities. The pain on his face was evident.

"As I was going to say, it seems I have a son. Over thirty-six years ago when I was a senior in college I had an affair with one of my instructors, Mrs. Amelia Broaii." Her dark faced paled at his remarks. "It seems that she became pregnant with my son..." Malcolm's voice caught at those words. "...and decided to raise him as the son of her husband. Now that he's deceased the truth is out. We have been tested, so now it seems that I am the father of three sons, Jacques, Mikal and Malcolm II." Cinnamon could see the relaxation that ran across Jock's brow. Mikal was a little harder to read. Black had raised him from age twelve and was known as his pops. At thirty-two he was a professor of African-American literature at Morehouse. Immediately the room was buzzing with activity as everyone stood embracing Malcolm. Cinnamon grabbed Jock, giving him a kiss and hug.

"Can I talk to you Mama C?"

"Of course..." taking his hand they walked outside to the balcony.

"Why didn't pops tell me before tonight?" She could hear the vibrant pain in his voice.

163

"Because he wanted to make sure, there was no point saying anything if it weren't true."

"So he didn't even know?"

"No baby he didn't know at all. The only thing that matters is that he loves you. I love you too, and when we get married you will sometimes stay with us."

"Are we still going on our vacation after Christmas?"

"Absolutely, you and me, pops and baby Amy."

"Okay…" She wrapped her arms around him.

"Can I get in on that?" Malcolm asked as he sat down between Cinnamon and Jock. He wrapped his arms around them both.

"Pops, am I still your favorite?" Cinnamon smiled at how young he sounded.

"Fo sho, my favorite boy, Amy is my favorite girl."

"Hey wait a minute…"

"Mama C, you his favorite woman…"

"Umm, okay…" The three of them laughed together.

"Come on let's get inside so we can eat."

The remainder of the evening was anti-climactic. It was clear everyone was struggling. Cinnamon noticed that Mikal, Sascha and Darrell had said very little to Malcolm II. Aura, Delia and Shelia had filled the void with conversation. They had all tried to engage Amelia but she stayed quiet with her eyes glued on her son or Malcolm when she thought no one was looking. Cinnamon and Malcolm sat quietly taking it all in with Amy lying across their laps.

Chapter Thirty Nine

"So how do you think things went?" Malcolm lay on the bed next to Cinnamon, his head resting on her stomach.

"Good. There are going to be some rippling effects. Mikal, Darrel and Sasha were all very quiet. Darrell because it took so long for him to get close to you, now that you and Brown aren't close anymore he cherishes his place as your closest male friend/brother. Mikal is harder to read, because he's no longer around but I suspect he's going to be a bit jealous also. Sasha doesn't really care one way or the other, so long as you keep her in cash." Black bellowed with laughter at her insight.

"You might be right on. What about Jock?"

"He's going to be okay. Jock only has two more years of high school, once he's gone to college, he won't be worried anymore. I'm most concerned about Amelia."

"Why?

"She watched you and Malcolm II all night. There's a great deal of tension between mother and son. And she couldn't keep her eyes off you. I don't want to have to beat her down."

"You would beat her down?"

"I'd beat her down to the ground!"

"I thought you were too cool for that."

"Boy, I have told you and told you not to let the smooth taste fool you. If she tries something with my man her butt is mine!" He fell out laughing, pulling her into his arms.

"She's not going to try anything. If she does, then I'll let you handle it."

"Don't think I won't."

"I know you will. So how is Brown?"

"As far as I know he's good. I don't talk to him. He was in town last month for Thanksgiving and Aura said he was fine. She talks to him at least once a week. Muha isn't talking very much to either of us. He's going to be at Aura's for Christmas Eve dinner. Is that okay with you?"

"Yeah it's cool. I have no problems with Brown. He just needs to not be putting his mouth all over you. I miss talking to him. When this thing came up with Malcolm II, I wanted to call him."

"You should have, you guys were very good friends, until Jezebel Cinnamon..."

"Stop that, we both fell in love with you at the same time. He got over thirty years, now I'm getting mine."

"Hmmm...Tomorrow I'm going to see Aunt Gladys, is it okay if I tell her about Malcolm II?"

"Well..."

"You already told her didn't you?"

"I did, I went by there the other day. I needed an elder and she's all the elder, both of us have. She could tell something was weighing on me. So I told her. She was as pleased as punch. I told her I was worried about how you would deal with it. She told me that you're a 'do or die chick'. I was surprised she knew what that meant." Cinnamon smiled inside.

"She spends too much time watching BET. She is right. I am do or die."

"And I love you for it…"

"That and the junk in my trunk…"

"Yes Lawd!"

Chapter Forty

"Hey Auntie Diva." Gladys was sitting on her sun porch reading her newspaper. Gladys loved bragging about her eyesight. Not bothering to tell people she wore contacts. She watched her niece walk up the sidewalk and thought she had never looked lovelier. That child had been through some trials but it was hard to see it on her. She walked onto the porch and immediately started kissing her aunt on the face before sitting down shoulder to shoulder with her.

"Hey baby, what's shaking?"

"But the bacon...what's shaking with you?"

"Nothing, just reading all this crazy news, sometimes I think about not reading it but I want to know. What's new?'

"Auntie Diva, quit playing, you know I got a thirty-five year old stepson." Gladys lifted her brow.

"Stepson, did you and Malcolm get married and not tell me?" Cinnamon smiled, she knew her aunt was mildly chastising her.

"No we didn't. I'm still sinning, though we will be getting married in March."

"March, huh. Now that another woman is on the scene, you decided you needed to hurry up and make that fine, sexy man legal?"

"Auntie you are too much. That might be part of it. But he's chomping at the bit and now with all this drama I thought it couldn't hurt to move the date up. We're going to have two ceremonies, one at the beach house and the other one in Jamaica with just the two of us."

"Sounds lovely, but don't worry about that man, he loves you and only you. So, what do you think of the boy and his mama."

"Malcolm II seems cool. The mama is hell on wheels, loves her some students. She's in her early sixties now. She still has a torch for Malcolm. I totally understand that. Any woman who has ever had his…"

"Cinnamon!"

"Uh sorry, I got lost for a minute." Gladys looked at her niece's flushed face and howled with laughter.

"You are sprung!"

"Auntie, I don't want you watching anymore BET. You know more slang than Muha."

"Speaking of Muha, how is he?"

"He's okay. He is still a little salty with me and very salty with his dad."

"Have you spoken to Brown?"

"Not in a few weeks, according to Aura he's doing well, still dating Mrs. Owa but Aura seems to think he has something else going on. Brown always liked sowing his oats and now that he is single he can literally make oatmeal."

"You don't care do you?"

"Not a twit. I loved him for years, he still has a place in my heart but I'm in love with one man and one man only and he's all I'm concerned about. It was hard trying to love two."

"I'm scared of you..."

"Now I know you cooked something so come on tell me what you got, so I can get some." Gladys stood up, walking inside with Cinnamon on her heels.

"Sit down, after you wash your hands I will serve you." Getting up to do as she was told, Cinnamon walked into the restroom. When she returned there was a fragrant bowl of short ribs with tomato, garlic and onions, ladled over basmati rice. Alongside that was a nice slice of homemade rosemary bread. Cinnamon rubbed her hands together in glee. Gladys smiled at her niece's enthusiasm. Her heart turned over at how she had been through so much and come through intact.

"Yummy, my favorites, please tell me you got more of this for me to take home."

"I made two batches. I have it already packed to send to your love den."

"Three months auntie, just three months…"
Cinnamon dove into her food.

Chapter Forty One

Walking into Aura's home with Black, Cinnamon felt a bit nervous. Last Christmas Eve she had still been married to Brown. She had noted his truck was parked in the driveway. Muha had informed her that he was having dinner with Amber and her family and would be home for New Year's. Though she would miss him she understood, he was a grown man and needed to make his own family. Glancing at Black she could see him watching her.

"Are you okay?" She looked lovely in a short black dress with ruby jewelry and muted makeup. He was just as handsome in black and burgundy.

"I'm wonderful. I just hope..."

"That me and Brown don't act a fool. Cinnamon I'm cool. I still love him and I'm sure he loves me. He just happens to love you and wishes you were still his wife."

"Well, I'm your wife..."

"That you are..."

Brown saw them walk in together, his heart turned over in his chest at how good they looked together. She looked especially beautiful. He was glad he had brought Khadijah with him. It didn't make it easy but it made it bearable. He stood up walking towards them. He pulled Black into an embrace, preparing to kiss Cinnamon. She made a point of turning her cheek to him. A shiver of pain ran through him but he understood.

"You two look good, like new money."

"You look good yourself Mr. Brown, all dressed up in blue." He was pleased to hear a bit of flirtation in her voice.

"Yeah man, you look sharp as hell. Is that a Mangini?"

"Yeah, it is, a brother has to always look his best, especially when he's over fifty and single." Khadijah chose that moment to appear at his side.

"Hello Mr. and Mrs. Black..." Cinnamon grinned inside. She knew Khadijah was making a point.

"March 15, now if you will excuse me, I'm going to talk to my daughter." Black and Brown watched her walk away. Khadijah watched them watching her. She decided to leave the men alone.

"Man, how is life treating you?" The two men walked outside. Sitting on the porch they had sat on many times over the years.

"It's good, different, not great but good. I don't have to ask you… so what's up. Darrell told me about your son." Black was a little surprised at that.

"Darrell told you. Hmm…yeah man I'm still trying to process it all. He is me all over. We're taking it easy. He's going to come by tomorrow and have dessert with Cinnamon and I."

"Wow… that must have been a shocker. It scared me."

"I'm sure…" The two men fell out laughing. It felt like the old days. Cinnamon's heart soared at the sound of the laughter and she immediately relaxed.

"So how does it feel?"

"Man, I don't even know. I'm still dealing with it. I wanted to call you when I found out."

"I wish you had. There are some things I don't want to talk to you about, but stuff like that we can always talk about. It's just too bad…"

"There couldn't have been two of her…"

"Yeah, something, like that."

"So what's up with Khadijah?"

"We cool. I think she wants to be Mrs. Brown, but it ain't happening, as hard as all this is, I love being footloose. I can sleep late, eat bad food and watch sports all day. I love it…sometimes…"

"How is Muhammad?"

"He's real pissed with me. At first he was mad as his mama, now he is mad at me. He seems ashamed of me." Black could hear the pain in Brown's voice.

"Man, in time it will be fine. He just needs to go through it. I have my problems with Mikal and Jock and I guess Darrell also, I'm going to talk to him tomorrow." The two men sat quietly lost in thought.

"Daddy, Step-D, it's time to eat." Aura's voice penetrated their consciousness. Black glanced at Brown to see how the Step-D affected him. Brown smiled at him as they stood to walk inside. The men sat at opposite ends of the table. Cinnamon sat next to Black. He looked at her, smiling, she wrinkled her nose at him. Brown swallowed down tears that sat on the edge of his lids. Khadijah stuffed food in her mouth, wanting to cry herself.

Chapter Forty-Two

The silence in the hotel room was palpable. Brown hadn't said a word to Khadiajh on the drive back. She thought maybe he would spend the night but he'd informed her he was going to stay with his daughter, he wanted to wake up with her and the baby on Christmas day.

"Did Aura not want me to stay?" Khadijah controlled the trembling in her voice.

"That is the home my wife and I lived in, of course you can't stay there."

"Then why can't you stay here with me."

"Because I want to be with my daughter and my grandchild, I need them,"

"William, will you ever love me?" Her voice was quiet and filled with pain. Brown turned from the window to look at her.

"Love you how? If you mean make love to you, go out with you, do things for you then yes I love you. But if you mean get married and share a home and accounts, I wish I could tell you that but I can't."

"So are you now going to be like Malcolm was for years? Will you have sex with women, with her on your mind and in your heart, hoping and waiting for her to become free again? She's happy William, she loves him and he loves her and they are going to be married. I don't say this to wound you, but I have never seen a happier couple." He swallowed down the bitterness her comments caused. There was nothing he could say because he had seen that with his own eyes. He also now understood how Black had felt all those years watching them together.

"Kadhijah, I really like you, a lot. But she was my life for so long. I just haven't dealt with this yet. I may never."

"If you loved her so much then why me and why the other women?" Tears sprung to his eyes.

"If I had the answer to that, then we wouldn't be here would we? I'll pick you up tomorrow. We are going to have dinner with my family, then get out of this damn town." He walked out without saying a word. She sat silently knowing she would take whatever he offered. She loved him, she hoped enough for them both.

*I'm going to have to really pray about all of this. I was doing fine but coming here and seeing them together was almost my undoing. They do look so damned happy. I can tell she still loves me, but him she...*Brown pounded his hands on the steering column in frustration. *Lord, please help me deal with this before I lose my mind.*

Chapter Forty Three

The next afternoon after visiting and eating with family members Cinnamon and Black sat on their porch, waiting for Malcolm II to arrive. They had a couple of hours. The morning had worn them out because they had separately and together tried to visit everyone. They sat side by side on the reclining chair, sipping tea.

"Black Man, are you nervous?"

"A little bit. Are you okay? I know today was tough without Muhammad and I suspect without Brown." She swallowed down the truth of his statement.

"Yeah, it was. I really miss Muha and I don't miss Brown per se, but he was a part of my life for so long. And as cool as he was last night I could feel his pain, especially at dinner, it vibrated off him. My heart also goes out to Khadijah, she's head over heels in love with him. I want him happy." She looked at Black to see if he understood. He smiled at her with love piercing his heart.

"I feel the same way and I would be shocked if you felt any differently. He was your husband for many years. That's why I stayed away for the past couple years. As bad as I wanted you, I needed it to be about your decision. I had given myself a timetable. I was going to wait until Jock graduated from high school then I was going to leave the country for a while." Shock and fear ran through Cinnamon. She was unable to control the tears that

179

fell from her eyes. Black wrapped his arms around her, holding her tightly.

"So you planned to leave me?"

"No baby, but the situation. I know I acted like what we were doing was okay, but sometimes it was killing me. Having you go against all you believed in to be with me and the toll it would take on you. Then there was the time you caught Brown with Khadijah, at that point I thought you would forgive him anything. That hurt down to my bones."

"You never let me see that."

"I couldn't afford to, I needed and wanted your decision to leave Brown to be yours. That's why I need to marry you."

"Eighty days..."

"Ummm, I suppose I can wait. That should give me enough time to resolve this baby daddy situation and try to soothe the ruffled feelings of my family. I hate to think it's true but I feel money is at the root of it." Shifting her body, she looked into the eyes of the man she adored. He smiled down at her.

"Of course it is. When I came in the picture, the money for them decreased exponentially. They have gotten used to me, now they have to deal with is blood thicker than blood issue. I just want to say don't even consider me in all of this. Together we have more than we will ever spend. All I want to do is grow old with you and our collective families and when I die, I don't care who gets what or does what with it."

"That's what I love about you. But I know what I plan to do and nothing will change that unless you go first. Then I will die anyway..." The two of them cuddled together, thinking about how all of this had transpired.

Chapter Forty-Four

Malcolm II arrived promptly at six. After serving dessert Cinnamon decided to go to her bedroom to read. She wanted Malcolm to work it out as he saw fit.

"So Malcolm, what are your expectations of me as your father." The younger man looked directly at his elder, his gaze never wavering. Malcolm was still startled at the resemblance.

"Sir, I have no expectations other than to have you in my life. I want to know you, be around you and have you visit me. I have a fiancé and one day I want a family, I would love for you to be a part of that. I have no ulterior motives. I know what you are worth and I know it serves you well to ask these questions. I will sign anything. I just want to know my…daddy." The sound of the word daddy hit Malcolm's heart like thunder. He never thought he would hear that word, from anyone. It took him several minutes to collect his thoughts.

"What about your mother?" A look of pain crossed the brow of the younger man.

"You will have to ask her, I can't speak for her. And she can't speak for me."

"That's fair. I will set up a time to speak to her."

"Sir, I have to get back to work tomorrow so I need to go home, but I would love to visit with you next week."

"Just let me know. The Center is closed until after the holidays. I might slip away with my love but I will keep in touch. Can I call you M2?"

"She is a lovely woman. And yes, I would love for you to call me M2, dad."

Black stood, pulling his son into a loving embrace. He held him for several minutes. Both men felt as though their hearts would explode. The younger man was concerned about his mother. He *KNEW* she had money on her mind. But he was resolved to allow his...daddy to handle it.

Malcolm stood in the room looking down at the love of his life, sleeping peacefully, he could only wonder how this had all transpired and thank God that it had. If he had written his own life story, this wouldn't be the case. He had never intended to tell her he was planning to leave one day. But he did because he now knew he didn't have to.

"What are you looking at?" Cinnamon's sleepy voice startled him from his thoughts. She pulled the covers back, allowing him to see she was in his favorite outfit, her lovely brown skin. He rushed over to get in beside her.

"So tell me how it went?" He nipped at the skin on her belly causing ripples of pleasure to flow through her.

"Maybe later..."

Chapter Forty-Five

Cinnamon walked through the marsh, looking out at the waves lapping up on the shore. She felt very much at peace. She also knew she was ready to marry Malcolm. She was simply waiting out of her fear not to allow Malcolm to control her, the way Brown once had. Thinking of Brown saddened her a bit. She knew he was enjoying his freedom, people talked and she didn't care. But, she really wished she weren't a factor for him. She knew he simply wanted things the way they had always been.

Walking inside she was startled by the ringing doorbell. Black had gone to talk to his brother and she didn't expect any visitors. She wasn't surprised to see Khadijah on her doorstep. Opening the door, she waved her in. Khadijah looked lovely in complete West African garb. Cinnamon smiled because she understood uniforms. Khadijah glanced at Cinnamon in a long black cotton and lace t-shirt dress and flip-flops. After sitting on the loveseat, she noted Cinnamon sat directly across from her.

"Well this is a surprise, how can I help you Mrs. Owa?" Cinnamon didn't offer drinks or food. She knew this wasn't a social call.

"Do you think he will ever let you go?" Cinnamon could see the pain, asking the question caused the older woman.

"Did you ask him?" Khadijah's gaze never wavered.

"I did, but Brown only says what he wishes to say. But, of course you know that."

"I do and I can't answer for him. My prayer is that he does let go. He needs to, I have."

"I could see that. Does it bother you that he's seeing me?"

"Not at all, I think it's perfect, because you know what you're getting. If you have plans to change him, my suggestion would be to not try it. I guess he will slow down one day..."

"But you weren't willing to wait for that?"

"Not any longer, once I fell in love with Malcolm, I knew then, but for whatever reason I hung on for a few more years. However, Brown decided to do something that I had asked him not to do. It was his decision."

"I don't suppose you want to tell me..."

"No ma'am I don't. You're going to have to work it out with him. I will tell you this... I'm not threat to you."

"Of course you are, in the same way you were a threat to every woman Malcolm was ever involved with. What is that you do, that you have?" Cinnamon giggled, then, laughed with glee for several minutes. Khadijah watched her with a perplexed look on her face.

185

"I wish I knew. If I did I would bottle it and sell it..."

"If you find out, please send mine express mail, COD." Surprised at Khadijah's ability to joke, Cinnamon laughed again, this time the other woman joined her. Standing to depart, she impulsively pulled Cinnamon into an embrace. She was pleased and surprised when the other women hugged her fully.

"I see why they love you..." Khadijah said before walking out the door, not looking back. Cinnamon wondered if Khadijah realized how much better she had made her feel. It freed her from concerns about what Brown did. He had to choose for himself. She ran upstairs to get ready for her day.

Chapter Forty-Six

Black walked into Restart. He was pleased that all the men were working and Darrell was the only one in the shop. He was pleased to see him with his feet on the desk, looking out the window. I meant that he finally felt the business was his.

"What up?" Darrell immediately took his feet off the desk as though he had been caught with his hand in the cookie jar.

"Man put your feet back up, this is your office. I'm just visiting. So what's going on?" Darrell relaxed, glancing at his brother, the man he admired most in the world.

"Not much, now. We as busy as heck around here these days. It feels good." Darrell had spent years, underemployed, but since Black had turned Restart over to him, he had been doing a wonderful job. Black sat down across the desk from his baby brother. He hadn't always been proud of him, but he was more than proud these days. He also knew he needed to get straight to the point.

"So what do you think of Malcolm II?" Immediately Darrell became wary.

"He seems alright, his mama is a mess. What was up with that?"

"Man, she was older and fine and after me. I simply accommodated her."

"I can't believe Mr. Safe Sex went in without protection?"

"Man, you know better than that. Sometimes condoms really do break." Malcolm didn't want to say that she had actually put the condom on him. He was now very suspicious. Though, he wasn't sorry about Malcolm II. "Now come on tell me what's up."

"I don't know what you mean?" Darrell wasn't quite looking at his brother.

"Man yes you do. When that man came in there, everyone was as cold as Antarctica. Josh at least admitted it. The only one who embraced him was Cinnamon."

"She embraces everyone. Besides, she knows where…"

"Where what?"

"Where she stands with you…"

"Man all of you should, ain't nothing changed in that way. And as for the money…" Darrell flinched at that, letting Black know he had hit a nerve.

"As to the money it's going to be the same…I have a designated amount of money that will go to my brother and sister and a designated amount that will go in equal parts to my children, Jock, Mikal and Malcolm II. He will get no more or less than those boys I raised. I'll also leave money for my nieces, nephews and Cinnamon's children in equal amounts. Everything else will go to my wife. If she passes before me then all of it will be divided up equally as noted above. And you know man, Restart is all yours, every bit of it." For several minutes the men sat quietly.

"Man, I'm sorry, but that isn't it, totally. I felt that someone else was going to come between us. In the past few years we have been real close. In many ways you have been my dad. It hurt me so bad when we weren't close. I don't want anything to mess that up." Darrell sounded embarrassed but Black's heart was filled.

"Man there is no chance of that. These days you are my main man." Darrell finally met his brother's eyes.

"And you mine, how are you and Brown getting along?"

"We cool. He is in a lot of pain and no one understands that better than me. I love him like a brother, but man I need her."

"I understand. It was a wise thing he moved."

"Yeah, it was… that was pretty much what kept me in New York for so many years. I just want to hurry up and marry her."

"What's the holdup?" Black grinned at his brother.

"She is exerting some personal authority. She feels she was controlled by Brown and she's going to show me what's up. She has moved the date up though. I think I can thank Amelia for that."

"Don't tell me the Queen is jealous."

"A little something, something, but I love it though. She ain't got a thing to worry about from me. Man all I want to do is love that woman. Once I marry her, I don't even plan to work at the Center but one day a month. The rest of the time I will be home waiting for her."

"Negro, you sound like a teenager in love."

"Man that's how I feel. People kill me thinking older people love differently. I'm marrying the woman of my dreams." Darrell was startled when his usually conservative brother stood up and starting doing the 'cabbage patch.' He wasn't sure what shocked him more, that he was doing it or how well he was doing it. He howled with laughter.

"I don't even want to know what ya'll do privately, to have you dancing like that!"

"And you won't either," Malcolm said as he moon-walked out the door." Darrell was amazed at how relieved he was, and it had nothing to do with money. Malcolm was also pleased. Now, he just wanted to get home to the woman who had him dancing.

Leaving the Center, Malcolm felt a sense of calmness about the family situation. He knew he still needed to speak to Mikal and Delia but that could wait. Mikal's feelings were probably bruised and he knew Delia didn't care one way or the other. She already had more money than she knew what to do with. Feeling the need for soul food Black pulled into the Soul Café. He knew Cinnamon was working at EP, he decided he would get plates for both of them, surprising her.

Standing at the counter, preparing to order his food, he felt arms surround his waist. The fragrance and body felt unfamiliar, so he turned to see who had the nerve to touch him. He was startled to see Amelia Broaii. Immediately he stepped out of her embrace, placing distance between them. A cryptic smile appeared on her face.

"So I make you flinch nowadays, is it because I'm an old woman, really old or is it because your sweet, young fiancé doesn't allow you to touch other women?"

"Amelia, I don't want to be touched by other women and I would thank you not to ever do that again." Glancing down at him, she smiled again.

"I guess I'm losing my touch. There was a time when you would have been visibly affected by my embracing you." Malcolm was startled by Amelia's flirtatiousness..

"Are you kidding me? There has been nothing between us in decades. At least nothing I knew about until recently." She flinched at the harshness in his tone. "Not only that but you have seen Cinnamon and you knew years ago that she was my only love. We didn't have a love relationship. We had sex!" Turning his back to her he picked up his food from the counter. The waiter was trying hard not to appear interested in what was being said. Amelia noted her lipstick on the back of his shirt and chose to say nothing. She did say as he brushed past her, "Malcolm we have a few issues to resolve, several thousand in fact." Fury pierced his brow but he didn't bother responding as he walked out the door.

It is time to call Aura Brown. She needs to get started on this. I want that woman paid and out of my hair. Damn! Pulling into the garage he could see Cinnamon's car was already inside. Glancing at his watch he realized it was later than he knew. Once inside he was glad he didn't smell food cooking. Walking into the bedroom he was pleased to see her pulling on her favorite lacy lounging dress. He was also pleased to see a smile on her face. He walked to her, pulling her into his arms.

"Hey baby, I brought dinner…"

"That's good, I'm very hungry and tired…" wrapping his lips around hers, he felt her surrender to his embrace, then he felt her body stiffening. Pulling back he noticed her nose was wrinkled.

"You smell funny. When you left this morning you smelled like Calvin Klein's Truth, now you smell like flowers…", she backed away looking at him quizzically. He knew it was Amelia's overpowering perfume. Before he could answer, she noticed the lipstick on the back of his shirt. He was startled when she ripped the shirt from his body, sending buttons flying. Thrusting the shirt into his face, she said in a deadly still voice,

"Malcolm Black, who has been kissing your back?"

"My back?" At that moment, he saw the red lipstick and remembered Amelia embracing him.

"Amelia, must have…"

"Amelia! You have thirty seconds to explain…" He could see the seconds, ticking off in her head. He had never seen her look more angry or beautiful. The color was amazingly high in her cheeks and her eyes were dark, flashing ovals. He was immediately filled with desire. He hurriedly explained to her what had happened, telling her that the waiter at the Soul Café could verify. Immediately the wind went of her sails and was replaced by embarrassment. Walking over he pulled her into his arms. His voice was low and husky.

"You owe me a shirt and an apology." Turning around, she not so gently slapped his face. She felt him becoming more turned on, and pulling her even closer. "Come on Cinnamon Bun, you better say sorry and promise to buy me a shirt or I'm going to make you pay for not trusting me."

193

"I will never apologize…" Her voice was now as low as his.

"You're going to make me spank you…"

"No one spanks Cinnamon…" He immediately pulled her into his lap, lightly tapping her bottom.

"No one…are you sure about that?" He was lightly tapping her bottom as he spoke, she was barely coherent…

"I was…

Chapter Forty Eight

Sitting on the floor at the foot of the bed, Malcolm and Cinnamon ate their very late dinner. He watched her devour her food.

"Have you eaten anything today?"

"I ate this morning, but being beaten and loved into submission will work up a sister's appetite." Malcolm howled with laughter as she placed a chunk of sourdough bread in her mouth.

"So I beat and loved you into submission..."

"You did and I'm going to tell my auntie...you know she will shoot anyone who messes with me." The two of them laughed again.

"Yeah, I heard. Please don't tell her, because if you do I won't do it again..."

"Yes you will..."

"Oh mighty sassy, now, aren't you? When you thought I was creeping, you were ready to beat me down, tearing my clothes off me..." Tears filled Cinnamon's eyes.

"I'm sorry..."

"Baby, don't be sorry, I love it when you're jealous and threatening violence. It's wonderful to have all that for me." She looked at him with a raised eyebrow.

"Really…I thought brothers hated drama…"

"Woman are you kidding, I want whatever you bring. Cinnamon, I have loved you since I was eighteen years old. When I have thought woman, wife, lover, friend, the only face I have ever seen was yours. And the fact that you are filled with violence is a very, sexy bonus. I love all of you, the light and the dark. The light makes you loving, the dark makes you loveable." Tears coursed down her face at his words, no one had ever said that. Most people including her parents and children had always run away when she got into one of her fits as they called it. They only wanted her at her best.

"Baby, why are you crying?"

"Black Man, those are tears of joy. Everyone has always found me to be too much work. Mama adored me, but she would get weird when I acted out as she called it. Brown couldn't stand it and it used to drive Aura insane. Muhammad was the only person who could deal with me when I had the 'blacks' as they called it. That's why I was so hurt by Muhammad earlier this year. He was always my ally."

"Well baby, I love it when you get the 'blacks.' Isn't that an ironic name for it, you certainly have Black, every bit of him."

"And for that I give thanks and praise everyday. It's nice to be able to act up. And since we're in that mode, what are you going to do about Mrs. Broaii?"

"I plan to talk to Aura tomorrow, to find out what she wants. If it isn't too ridiculous, I plan to give it to her. But I first I want to know what Malcolm II wants me to do. Maybe I can give it to him."

"Umm umm, though I'm sure he will give it to her, but in order for her to understand this is a one time deal, give it to her making sure she signs a document of understanding. Then whatever you want Malcolm to have, give it to him, personally. Don't have him deal with that. My suggestion is offer her 300K, that is 15K a year times eighteen years plus interest. As for college funds, my understanding is he had full scholarships and incurred no expenses to his family. However, he did work so offer to give him whatever he earned during those years. That could really help with his business." This time tears filled his eyes.

"That's why I love you so much. Will you handle this for me?"

"Absolutely, tell Aura what to do. I'll meet with Mrs. Broaii. Do you plan to be there?"

"Not unless you want me there. I would prefer not to deal with her."

"Then, I will certainly handle it. Now come on, I want some ice cream in bed." He followed her, his heart filled with love.

Brown has got to be the biggest fool I know. But I thank God for his foolishness. A beautiful, sexy woman who knows how to handle things, who could ask for more?

Chapter Forty-Nine

Cinnamon prayed on the way to Aura's office. Amelia Broaii had stalled for a week before finally agreeing to a meeting. She still wasn't aware that Malcolm wouldn't be in attendance. She thought she was meeting with him and Aura. She had refused initially because she felt Aura was biased. She was in for the surprise of her life. Cinnamon had asked Malcolm if he had changed his mind about coming. He had simply nodded no, telling her how much he loved her. He also reminded her that March was only two and a half months away.

"Hey baby..." Aura watched her mom walk in dressed in dark gray cashmere. She knew when Cinnamon got dressed to the nines she was preparing to do battle. Her short black and silver curls glistened, and her makeup was minimal, however, her lips were fire engine red. The soft woman that usually shone through was nowhere on display. Pride pierced Aura's heart and a bit of pain. For years she had failed to see her mother's strengths, judging her by what she considered her 'sexy femininity,' not realizing her mother was stronger and tougher than all of them. She simply knew how to pick her battles.

"Hey mama, you look fierce..." Before Cinnamon could answer, Amelia Broaii walked into the office. It was clear she was looking for Malcolm as she glanced around the office.

"Amelia, please have a seat, Malcolm won't be joining us." Not quite looking at Cinnamon, Amelia asked why.

"Because his appearance isn't necessary, Aura has drafted a package for you to read and then sign. You are also welcome to have an attorney read it, however I feel it is more than fair, considering." Aura was impressed by the professional tone her mom used, Amelia appeared to be intimidated. She was still standing and Cinnamon in her three inch heels was easily six inches taller. Finally, she sat down, pulling the two paged document from the table. For thirty minutes the room was quiet and still as Amelia read and reread the documents. She placed them on the table, folding her arms. Refusing to acknowledge Cinnamon she directed her look at Aura.

"So what happens if I refuse to sign the document?" Aura glanced at Cinnamon, who replied, "Then you will get nothing, two-hundred thousand tax free dollars is extremely generous." She had rethought the figures. "There is no court in this country that would award you a dime. In fact there are attorneys who would encourage Malcolm to sue you for denying him access to his son for over thirty years. So, my advice to you would be to sign the document, take the check and allow the Malcolms to develop their own relationship." Aura watched with fascination, she had never seen the business side of her mom, but, she knew this was more than business.

"Are you warning me Mrs. Brown?"

"Not at all, I'm simply telling you from the one side that the men need to deal with their own relationships. Malcolm II is a grown man. And from the personal tip, I am telling you the other Malcolm is not available." Aura held back a chortle; her mom was more impressive by the minute. Amelia nodded, took the pen she had been offered and signed the documents. When she was done, Cinnamon handed her a check, written on her personal account. Amelia looked at the check and then back at the woman who handed it to her.

"Point taken." Sliding the check in her purse, she hurried from the room. Aura's laughter erupted as soon as she was gone.

"Woo, I wouldn't want to come up against you in a courtroom. Muhammad is right, you are a gangster. I loved that personal part. Lady you are fierce." Cinnamon pulled her daughter into an embrace, swallowing back tears, thinking of all the years she had sucked down what she really felt. Aura pulled back, looking at her mom.

"Cinnamon Bun, are you okay?"

"I'm awesome. Just glad I don't have to hide my power any longer." Aura smiled proudly at her mom.

"Come on Diva, let's go to Morton's and eat medium rare steak, crème brulee and drink a bottle of champagne."

"Make it a bottle and a half and I'm in.

Chapter Fifty

Malcolm paced around the house waiting for Cinnamon. He had been expecting to hear from her for hours. He had called her cell phone and gone by EP and no one had seen her. He had also tried to get in touch with Aura and she hadn't answered her phone. After checking their joint account no money was gone, so he was worried that Amelia had been a problem. He had gone so far as to call her and she had told him to check with his fiancé before hanging up in her ear. Glancing outside for the fiftieth time, he saw Cinnamon getting out of Aura's car with her shoes in her hands, singing, *"I am every woman'*, at the top of her lungs. Aura looked amused. When they reached the porch, he realized that Cinnamon was drunk. Completely sloshed and Aura wasn't far behind her. Trying to hide his shock, Black looked at Aura, who shrugged her shoulders. Cinnamon was still singing. She fell into his arms giggling. He sat down on the chaise, pulling her onto his lap. Almost immediately she was snoring softly. Aura was sitting on the chaise next to him.

"Hey Step-D, me and mama had a lot of champagne, a lot."

"No kidding…what's going on…?"

"We were celebrating. I'll let mama tell you. Can I take a nap?" Before he could answer she was sleeping. He gently took Cinnamon inside, placing her in bed. When he got back to the porch, Aura had curled up in a ball and was snoring gently. Smiling, he covered her with a blanket and went inside to prepare a meal for his women.

"Oooh, my head hurts." Malcolm glanced at Cinnamon. It was three o'clock in the morning. She had been sleep for nine hours. Aura had woken after a couple hours and had dinner with him. He still didn't know what happened with Amelia. Placing her feet on the floor Cinnamon felt the room spin. Malcolm made his way over to her.

"I really should spank you for this…" She could hear the laughter in his voice.

"Okay but could I take a bath and have a sandwich first?" Nodding at her he walked from the room. She went in the bathroom, filling the tub with lemongrass oil and warm water. She felt immediately better once she was up to her neck in the fragrant water. Within minutes Malcolm walked in with a turkey sandwich and a cup of green tea. He pulled off his clothes, getting in with her.

"Now tell me what happened." After eating half her sandwich, Cinnamon replied.

"Aura didn't tell you?" Malcolm lifted his eye with mock exasperation.

"Oh okay. Well Amelia signed the documents. I gave her check for 200K and she went on her way."

"Just like that? I didn't see any funds transfers." Cinnamon sipped her tea before answering.

"Yeah, just like that. I also told her to stay away from my man…"

"Did you now, now what about the funds? I thought you were going to do a direct deposit?"

"I gave her a check, a check from me…"

"What does that mean?"

"It means I gave her a check from my personal account." Tears filled Malcolm's eyes.

"Why?"

"Because I wanted to and it was a wedding present to you…since we are getting married tomorrow…"

"Tomorrow?"

"Umm hmm, Aura and I arranged it before we got drunk…" Malcolm stood up in the water and started dancing around, screaming at the top of his lungs, "Yes! Yes! Yes! Cinnamon watched him with joy in her heart. He picked her up swinging her around. Water splashed everywhere. "Finally, you are going to be mine, all mine…no more sinning!" Laughter rang out in the bathroom.

"So can we go consummate this thing…?"

"Oh no ma'am, I'm not fornicating with you any more. The next time you get this, you will be Mrs. Black." Looking at him, Cinnamon could see he was serious. Her heart turned over at the love.

"Then you need to cover all that up before I make you forget yourself." He jumped from the bathtub, running from the room. Cinnamon sat for several minutes with a smile on her face.

Thank you God for this, I know we didn't go about this the right way, but God I love her and she loves me and we will grow in your word together, forever. Amen. Malcolm Black was as happy as he had ever been. He had the woman of his dreams, finally, and a son to carry on his name. God is Good.

LaVergne, TN USA
19 January 2010
170533LV00002B/54/P